For more than forty years,
Yearling has been the leading name
in classic and award-winning literature
for young readers.

Yearling books feature children's
favorite authors and characters,
providing dynamic stories of adventure,
humor, history, mystery, and fantasy.

Trust Yearling paperbacks to entertain,
inspire, and promote the love of reading
in all children.

OTHER YEARLING BOOKS YOU WILL ENJOY

QUiT iT

Marcia Byalick

A YEARLING BOOK

To my husband, the keen observer,
whose back hurts every time he sees
someone carrying a heavy burden

Published by Yearling, an imprint of Random House Children's Books
a division of Random House, Inc., New York

Visit us on the Web! www.randomhouse.com/kids

Educators and librarians, for a variety of teaching tools, visit us at
www.randomhouse.com/teachers

ISBN: 0-440-41865-8

Reprinted by arrangement with Delacorte Press

Printed in the United States of America

February 2004

10 9 8 7 6 5 4 3 2

OPM

1

Is there a dumber question in the universe than "How was school today?" It wouldn't be so bad if the person asking actually cared about the truth. But the only answer people really want to hear is "Fine." Especially if they're part of your family.

"So, Clementine, how was school today?" my mom asked my sister as she passed the mashed potatoes.

Life could be worse, I thought. I could have been born first. Then *my* name would be Clementine instead of Carrie. My fingers started tapping the table, the way they do every night, leaving the place where I sit pockmarked like the wood had a bad case of acne. From the corner of my eye, I noticed my mom staring down at her plate, trying hard to hide her irritation.

Lately she'd given up biting her bottom lip or making remarks like "Are you sure you can't stop tapping, darling . . . at least until after dinner?" I so would prefer her just saying what's on her mind: "STOP MAKING THAT SOUND. . . . IT'S DRIVING ME CRAZY!" Not that I could stop, of course.

"It sucked," my sister mumbled, finally answering the question, her mouth full of broccoli. This month she was on a fighting-cancer kick. Her diet consisted mostly of green, smelly steamed vegetables. It was better than the month last year when she ate only white things . . . rice, vanilla ice cream, and white bread.

Clementine is a junior in high school, and she's the kind of person who never does anything she doesn't want to do. She ignores fashion magazines, insisting that popular kids all look the same. If you think clothes are important, she'll say, then they become the boss of you. Her favorite bands have names nobody ever heard of and look like they just fell out of bed and realized they were out of toothpaste. If you don't like her taste, her friends, her hair, she couldn't care less.

Me, on the other hand, I care too much. I swallowed hard and tried to stay calm. Sometimes if I think happy thoughts, I'm able to keep my tics from ending the dinnertime conversation. Only sometimes.

"You know that sign I put up in my room last week?" my sister asked. "I think it worked."

Clementine is always putting up signs in her

room. Just yesterday she taped a new one on her door. It said HEROES WHO NEVER GRADUATED FROM COLLEGE. So far, she has only five names on it: Thomas Edison, Babe Ruth, Bill Gates, Queen Elizabeth, and Al Fields. Al Fields is my grandpa. I think she does things like that just to drive my parents crazy.

"What sign was that?" my father asked as he sort of eye wrestled with my mother, begging her not to say anything, no matter what was coming.

Wedged between her posters of Bob Marley and Mia Hamm, Clementine had scribbled the number ninety-six on a plain piece of loose-leaf paper. We all saw it, but no one was brave enough to ask her what it meant.

"I read if you write down what you want and you look at it every day, you're bound to get it. That ninety-six was what I wanted to get on my math exam. I had the test today. And I think it worked."

Just like that. Not because she studied or is good in math. She's convinced she does amazing because she reads the number ninety-six every day. Trust me, we're a normal Long Island family. It's hard to figure how my sister got so strange.

My father is a lawyer. He has to care about what other people think. My mother still talks about how she used to be a cheerleader in high school, so you know she's definitely into how people see her. We have two cars, four TVs, three phones, and a cat. Not exactly the ideal breeding ground for raising a free spirit like Clementine.

"How was your day?" I asked my mother. My throat pulsed with the coughs I was working so hard to keep inside.

"Hectic," Mom sighed. "It's like all of a sudden the whole world is having chest pains." Mom works as the office manager for three cardiologists. Not only does she know every patient by name, she knows all of their life stories. If we ever run into one at the supermarket, she'll tell me if he or she still smokes, if the patient's job is particularly stressful, or if he cheats on his diet and eats hot dogs. She cares about every single one of them and gives out advice as if she's part of the medical team.

That's what makes it so bizarre when she acts as if nothing is wrong with me.

• • •

Last May or June, I started to blink. I mean really blink, with both eyes, like fifty times a minute. Once it started, there was no way I could stop until my eyes themselves decided to quit. It was annoying to me, but it drove my mom crazy. The first thing she did was cut my bangs. When that didn't work, she cut them shorter. For weeks I walked around looking like a blinking freak with a huge forehead. I told her ten times my bangs had nothing to do with the problem. When she saw I was right, she took me to an eye doctor. I got these cool glasses; Clementine helped me pick them out, and my eyes relaxed back to normal.

About a week later, I started clearing my throat. You know how it feels when you have a tickle? Well, no matter how many times I tried clearing my throat, I couldn't get that tickle to go away. It was like the blinking but worse, because now I made noise. I tried to keep it down but everyone around me heard. It was the worst when I went to the library or got into an elevator, where it was quiet. People would check me out, then pretend not to notice. Sometimes they'd look at each other, then back at me, then shrug or roll their eyes. Right in front of me. Like I was blind. Like I was invisible.

Mom went to Price Club and bought home huge cases of all kinds of lozenges. I sucked my way through seven boxes a day, but I still kept clearing my throat. Then miraculously the tickling disappeared. Although he never came out and said the noise bothered him, Dad was so relieved when it stopped, he took me for ice cream and acted as if I were responsible for making it go away.

After only a few weeks, I started sniffing. I don't know how to explain it. It was like a witch put this curse on me. I couldn't stop smelling everything. Because it sounded like my nose was running, I made believe it was stuffed up. I knew it wasn't a cold or allergies, but I'd fill my pockets with tissues and blow and blow and act like something came out. Then I'd dump fistfuls of dry, wadded-up Kleenex in the first garbage pail I passed and start all over again.

Mom took me to an ear, nose, and throat doctor. He looked in, up, and around every hole in my face but couldn't find anything wrong. I think that's the afternoon, in his office, when the head jerking began. Out of the blue I couldn't keep myself from turning my face to the left, then back again. Like some alien had invaded my body and was giving it instructions without my permission. The doctor glanced at my mother and wrote down the name of a neurologist he said might be able to help.

My mom's silences are so loud. She didn't say one word the whole ride home that day. Or the afternoon two months later when the blood tests the neurologist took came back negative, ruling out a dozen things it might have been, leaving only one possibility. It took three months, three doctors, and the process of elimination to give what was wrong with me a French name. It was kind of pretty actually, Tourette Syndrome. The strange things I was doing were called tics. The diagnosis left most every question we had unanswered. The doctor said there was no telling when new tics might crop up. He didn't know why I got them and he couldn't say if or when they would ever disappear.

Fortunately, there was medicine. September was only weeks away and the last thing I wanted was to tic my way through middle school. Unfortunately, after ten days I had to stop taking the pills the doctor prescribed. They made me so groggy I couldn't concentrate. By eleven-thirty in the morning, I needed a nap. The doctor called in a different prescription when new, even weirder symptoms appeared, but that pill was worse than the first one. An hour after I took it, it felt like it was the middle of the night. Once I fell asleep during lunch and my mom had to come to my friend Amy's house and take me home. Another time I had to miss my favorite dance class because by three o'clock I couldn't wait to crawl upstairs to bed. I would have gladly tried anything . . . even if it had to be injected into my arm every day, like the medicine my aunt Rose takes for her diabetes . . . anything to make life return to how it was. But there was no such magic potion, at least not for me.

It was about that time I stopped seeing Amy and Whitney. The three of us had been best friends all through elementary school. I knew they weren't trying to be mean or anything, but there was no doubt my tics freaked them out. Whenever I sniffed or coughed too many times in a row, I saw them exchange a look that made me feel lonelier than I can ever remember. It wasn't their fault. Three is always a tricky number when it comes to friendships. After I made some lame excuses two Saturdays in a row about why I couldn't see them, they stopped calling. It was just easier.

I wouldn't exactly say Dad blamed me when I went off the medication, but I knew he'd rather see me be sleepy than be so annoying. I wanted to ask him if he thought I'd rather be humiliated every single day, fifty times a day, than take a pill to make the symptoms go away. I wanted to explain that starting seventh grade was hard enough without feeling like you were walking through ten feet of water. That if he hated to see how each new tic looked and sounded, he should spend a day catching the view from my vantage point, under my skin. But I didn't.

"I have to go up and finish my homework," I said loudly, interrupting the tale of how Mr. Schweiger drove himself to the emergency room in the middle of a heart attack.

Mom nodded. Parents never argue if you use homework as an excuse. They didn't want to hear about my disastrous day anyway. Besides, if I said my brain felt like it was going to explode, they'd say no it doesn't. They're like that. So I figure the less they know, the better.

They can't help me anyway. Nobody can.

2

Nobody is ever ready for the summer to end. But for a kid newly diagnosed with Tourette, it can make you nauseous: you worry about sitting still, disturbing the class, annoying your teachers, and a million other possible humiliating moments. What made it even harder was as much as I dreaded reentry into the real world, I couldn't wait to get it over with. To be honest, up to that point in my life, nothing was ever as horrible—not a test or a shot or one of Clementine's boring orchestra concerts—as my imagination anticipated it would be. I prayed that going back to school would be like that, awful to think about but not so bad once it happened.

My mother had gone up to school before the first

day to alert the principal, the school psychologist, the school nurse, and my teacher, Mrs. Davis, that I would be joined this year by an assortment of habits guaranteed to irritate anyone within range. She never told me what she said or what they said and I didn't ask. Worst come to worst, I figured they'd feel sorry for me. And if that would help, I wasn't too proud to accept their pity.

The person who came up with the expression "your worst nightmare" must have been sitting in my seat those first few weeks in seventh grade. I concentrated so hard on keeping still and staying quiet that I hardly paid any attention to what was going on. I'm sure everyone thought I was snobby and unfriendly, but I was afraid if I loosened up, I'd unleash a torrent of tics. As it was, the kids sitting near me stared at the fraction of those head movements that escaped. Not one asked any questions or made any comments. I guess I was glad about that.

Although Mrs. Davis never made any specific reference to me, she made a big deal about what she called "civility," treating people the way we wished they'd treat us. She had no patience for rudeness of any kind—mean jokes, pushing on line, or name-calling—and could be tough on any kid caught picking on someone. Once, the first week, I noticed her shooting some hard looks at a few kids sitting behind me. I turned just in time to catch two boys mimicking my neck moves, jerking their heads in unison. As I turned my red-hot face back to the front of the room, I watched Mrs. Davis stare them down, having an entire angry, threatening conversation with her eyes. That stare was powerful, and they never bothered me again.

As the weeks went by, I grew exhausted from the effort of holding everything inside. The moment I let go, just a bit, my odd behaviors became more obvious. Mrs. Davis was cool about letting me take my time finishing up tests. She never yelled if my work was sloppier than it should have been and she didn't care if I stood next to my desk for as long as I needed to when I couldn't bear sitting anymore. I didn't have to ask permission or explain. Every once in a while I'd catch her watching me with her eyebrows all knit together as if she were trying to work out a problem. As soon as she'd catch me looking at her, she'd wink and smile. That's how I know she felt bad for me.

I guess I should be grateful for how quickly my tics became old news to the rest of the class. It made me think of what living across from the train station or next door to the airport must be like, when after a while you don't hear a thing. While in my heart I felt like there was a huge floodlight shining directly on me every time I twitched, my brain understood that no one was paying any attention. They didn't mock me; they didn't sympathize; they didn't care.

• • •

My grandma says friends are the chocolate chips in the cookies of life. If that's true, then Clyde Paskoff is the biggest chip in my cookie. He's been my best friend ever since I sat next to him in nursery school. I remember him raising his little four-year-old hand when the teacher asked what we would do if our houses were on fire. "Stop, drop, and roll!" he yelled before falling to the floor, just as he had seen on a public-service announcement on television. That pretty much explains my friend Clyde. The teacher wanted us to say we would run out of the house and call 911. But Clyde always acts as if his clothes are on fire.

I was the one who calmed him down in second grade when he came into school worried about "cereal killers." He'd heard on the news that there was a manhunt throughout Long Island for a guy who had murdered more than twelve people. The announcer on television called him a serial killer, and in Clyde's mind, there was a murderer on the loose who was after anyone who had Cheerios for breakfast.

Clyde would be the best person to sit next to on a plane. He's the only kid I know who listens to every single word a flight attendant says when she gives out instructions before takeoff. He always memorizes where the emergency exits are and is completely prepared to strap on his oxygen mask and flotation device if need be. In the last year alone, Clyde lost sleep about the flesh-eating Ebola bacteria, the picture of the girl who hung upside down on a roller coaster for three hours in North Carolina, and whether, by the time we get there in a few years, Hillside High School will have metal detectors to keep out trench-coat-wearing crazies who bring guns to school. It's like poor Clyde is always swimming in an ocean of viruses.

For the past few weeks, Clyde had been in a life-

or-death struggle with a different kind of killer. She weighed only one milligram and lived only a week. She came from Africa, and scientists didn't have a clue how she got here or why she was flying around our neighborhood. Every moment of Clyde's life was filled with tension because he believed it was only a matter of time before she'd find him. And bite him. And give him a life-threatening disease that attacks the brain.

"These mosquitoes, they suck the blood out of dead, infected birds," he whispered during lunch one day. "First they carry it in their gut. Then the blood gets into their salivary gland. Then they shoot it into us."

"What, did you read a textbook? How do you know all this?" I asked calmly, gearing up to deal with the latest dark cloud hovering over my friend's head. How I wished he could have gotten through another summer like last year, when he was ignorant about West Nile virus, when he wore T-shirts and shorts, before he was obsessed with his brain being devoured by mosquitoes.

"One mosquito can lay one hundred eggs in a pond or a birdbath or a flowerpot. Even a big puddle. Ten days later, they hatch, start to fly, and begin to hunt for blood," he went on. "If one bites you, the virus drives through the three layers that cover your brain and turns it to deadwood."

"You watch too much television." I sighed. "Look around. Does anyone look scared? If your parents thought you were in danger, wouldn't they do something to protect you?"

But I knew nothing I could say would make him feel any better. He wouldn't care that the chances of his being bitten were ridiculously small, or that so far, the ten people who had died from encephalitis were all over sixty years old. My mother once said that parents can only be as happy as their unhappiest child. Now, even though Clyde wasn't my son, I was beginning to understand what she meant. I hated the nightly news for spoiling the best time of the year for Clyde, and consequently for me.

"Don't you ever read the paper?" he said with disgust. "I'm not making this stuff up. I'm telling you, if your neck starts to feel stiff, you'd better call the doctor. In a few hours you can slip into a coma."

Clyde should know that mosquitoes don't frighten me. In fact, for almost a year now, the idea of being in a coma has sounded pretty good. If you're unconscious, you don't worry what new, embarrassing symptom is on its way to ruin your life. You can't think about how it makes you go nuts inside if you don't avoid every crack in the sidewalk. So nuts, in fact, that sometimes you wind up walking back and forth down the same block four times to make sure. So that no matter what time you leave the house in the morning, chances are you're going to be late for school.

If you're not awake, you can't do stuff that doesn't make any sense, like checking your book bag ten times to make sure you have your homework. Or having to knock on the kitchen table exactly thirty times before getting up from a meal. Or needing to count how many words are on each line as you read, so you can't keep up with the class.

It was amazing how Clyde pulled himself together to help me deal with my Tourette. He found its wild, uncontrollable symptoms fascinating. He even said it made me the most interesting person he'd ever met. Besides, he laughed, it was about time he had a turn to play the normal friend.

From the beginning he was the only one who wasn't afraid to talk to me about it. He asked a million questions and tried to make me laugh. "Turn off your nose, it's dripping," he'd say after seeing me stuff a thousand empty tissues in my desk. The joke was older than America, but it made me smile.

Clyde knows how much I love writing on a clean, fresh, white page. It has always been important to me to be neat. Now sometimes when I had to copy stuff from the chalkboard, I'd get so frustrated from falling behind to count the words on each line that I'd rush and make mistakes and erase and rip my paper. He went out with his mom and bought this special stuff at Staples. If he put it underneath his sheet, it made two copies of what he wrote. Then he gave me the second copy so I could write it over slowly at home. I told you he's a good friend.

We're aliens, Clyde and me. On the outside we get good grades, appear in every school play, are pretty decent soccer players, and are sensational at Game Boy. On the inside we're scrambled eggs.

3

The minute I saw her standing at the front of the classroom, I knew it was going to be a bad day. I'm not saying I think all substitute teachers are evil, but whenever I have to disguise my tics in front of a stranger, chances are it will not be a positive experience.

Mrs. Harris is large and soft, like a pillow. She uses words like "hush" and "smitten" and always has lipstick on her teeth. It's easy for the kids to take advantage of her. She knows it too. Her shoulders are scrunched right up to her ears, as if she's constantly on the alert, waiting to be attacked.

She didn't have long to wait.

"Mrs. Davis doesn't give us homework on Wednesdays," called out Jesyca in her best fake, trying-to-be-helpful voice. The idea wasn't bad, but her timing was dumb.

It was only 9:02.

"It's hot in here," Michael added from the back of the room. "Mrs. Davis always lets us open the window when it's this warm."

I saw Clyde stiffen immediately.

Jesyca nodded vigorously, as if Mrs. Harris would definitely believe Michael if she agreed. On the list of things Jesyca does best, nodding is second only to tossing her hair.

When Jesyca reads out loud, she sounds as if she is reciting her lines, front and center, in the middle of a Broadway stage. She's the only girl in the class with long, curly hair. Every single day she wears a belt, which she says reminds her to have good posture. She says she doesn't own a sweatshirt—how weird is that? Instead, she tucks tiny, shiny, silky tops into her skinny jeans, in spite of the fact she brings Doritos and Reese's Pieces every day for a snack. Jesyca's never actually done anything bad to me, but you can understand why sometimes she's hard to like.

Clyde's whole body was now tensed up like a cricket. With the window open, no telling how many disease-carrying mosquitoes would fly into the room. He searched through his desk, stuffed something in his pocket, then stood up and walked to the door. That was the procedure when someone had to go to the bathroom.

He stood there while Mrs. Harris took attendance.

And while she wrote ten math problems on the board for us to copy. She said if we did these quickly and quietly she would consider the homework request.

Clyde raised his hand, but of course she couldn't see because her back was to the door.

"Excuse me, I'm sorry to bother you, but I really have to go." He spoke fast, as if to convince Mrs. Harris this was really an emergency.

Poor Clyde looked like his life was in jeopardy. I didn't know where he was going, but I knew his heart was probably jumping up and down in his chest like popcorn in a microwave.

"We stand at the door when we want to be excused," I said loudly. "Mrs. Davis always lets us go."

Then I cleared my throat.

Mrs. Harris turned around to see who was talking. Then she glanced down at her watch. She made a face, letting Clyde know she didn't think he should be leaving the room so early.

I cleared my throat again. It sounded like I had something else to say.

She looked up questioningly.

Of all the tics in my grab bag of nodding, gulping, flinching, and head jerking, my brain had to pull out throat clearing. I lowered my head and bit my lip, trying not to make any more noise so she would just let Clyde go.

"All right then, make sure you don't dally and come right back."

Dally? Exactly how does one dally? Another time I would have tried to catch Clyde's eye. But her tone was stern and I didn't want her to think we were trying to make trouble.

Clyde raced out the door. The class was silent, copying the math problems on the board.

I cleared my throat once more, then again. At that moment I wished myself out the window, across the schoolyard, down three blocks, in my bedroom, under my covers.

"Well, since you seem to want my attention, it's all yours." Mrs. Harris put down the chalk and walked up the aisle to my seat. She stood in front of me and folded her arms. My luck. She thought I was a wise guy, that I was testing her.

Everyone stopped writing and watched me.

I pretended to be so busy working on a math problem, I didn't notice her standing there. She smelled extremely minty, like she bathed in Listerine. I tried to concentrate on how uneven my columns of numbers looked. Not one example lined up properly. In the heading alone, there was a smudge the size of a gum ball. The whole page was horribly sloppy. In a panic I started to erase every one of the five problems I'd finished. The paper ripped in half.

Someone snickered. I wiped my eye quickly with my arm, doing it sort of casually, as if I had a sweaty brow or something. I prayed it would hide the fact that now the sounds coming from my throat were accompanied by my head jerking furiously in Mrs. Harris's direction. I looked up, ready to apologize, to explain I really wasn't trying to annoy her.

But Mrs. Harris was backing away. Suddenly,

instead of being angry with me, she looked uncomfortable. My behavior was scaring her. The poor woman didn't know what to do with me.

"Carrie's not trying to be funny. She has these tics she can't stop," sang out a voice from the back of the room. It sounded as if she were reading out loud, projecting her voice to the last row of the balcony. It could only be the hair-tossing queen. "Mrs. Davis usually just ignores her."

I turned around to see Jesyca standing proudly at her seat, beaming one of her super-deluxe phony smiles right in my direction. As Clementine would say, she was far from the brightest crayon in the box. Completely clueless, she expected me to be grateful to her for rescuing me.

Flush-faced, Mrs. Harris returned to her desk without a word.

The door opened. Clyde glanced at me and returned to his seat. He had taken off the windbreaker he wore tied around his waist and put it on, covering his arms. He had wet his hair to remove any smell of shampoo. And wherever he walked, a thick haze of insect repellent followed.

4

It wasn't even ten o'clock and the day was a disaster.

Then it got worse.

I heard it first. It sounded like an old refrigerator. Then there it was, moving slowly, like a plane circling the airport. It was the fattest, hairiest black fly I had ever seen. It buzzed around, flitting about the height of the closet, looking like it was too heavy to climb any higher.

I shot Clyde a look, hoping he didn't see him yet. Yeah, right, like that would ever happen. Clyde had extrasensory radar to alert him when any one of the hundred things that scared him came near. He was already bent over, pulling up his socks. Somehow, in a split second he had buttoned the top button on his polo shirt. And he was sweating.

I had to make eye contact with him. For someone who was so smart about everything that can kill you, how could he not know this was no mosquito? I decided to write him a note: DON'T WORRY. IT'S DEFINITELY A BOY. I PEEKED! YOU SAID THE MALES DON'T BITE, RIGHT?

Luckily, he was close enough for me to heave it underhand right onto his desk. He read it and smiled weakly.

I shot him one of my bossy you're-being-ridiculous, calm-down looks. It didn't work. Sometimes when you're afraid, even the facts don't help.

I raised my hand. And blew my nose loudly with the other hand.

Mrs. Harris swallowed hard.

"I have bad allergies. And April is the worst month. Could you please shut the window?"

I faked an excellent coughing fit.

"Yes, of course," she said, getting up immediately and shoving the window closed.

Okay. At least no more monster flies would lumber in. Now all I had to do was get rid of the pesky buzzard overhead. Ordinarily I'm not a violent person, but in this case there was no other solution. Not that Clyde would agree. As much as he despises mosquitoes, he could never kill one. He never even blows on ladybugs.

The fly buzzed about in slow motion as if he were reading the posters Mrs. Davis had all over the room. He landed atop the "L" on the HAPPINESS IS LEARNING sign, then made his way past WHEN YOU BELIEVE IN YOURSELF, ANYTHING IS POSSIBLE. He lunged toward A GOOD BOOK IS A GOOD FRIEND, ignoring WE CAN ALL LEARN FROM EACH OTHER.

I planned my strategy. As soon as Godzilla landed, I would walk over and smash him with my math book. Mrs. Harris already thought I was crazy, and besides, it would be a done deal by the time she realized what had happened. She droned on about the earth and the moon and gravity while I kept my eye on Clyde's lazy enemy. I glanced over to see Clyde clutching his pencil, as if praying for something to write to keep his mind off his troubles. In that second, I lost sight of the fly.

No one else in the class seemed aware of the fly . . . or his imminent fate. Suddenly I saw him creeping across Michael's sneaker. Then he made a short hop over to dawdle on Lara's book bag. He was about to inch down into the bag when he changed his mind, or whatever flies change, and flew off in a different direction.

My heart quickened. I tried to ignore the stiffness in my neck signaling the beginning of a wicked head-jerking attack. I couldn't lose focus. He was crawling on the floor, coming my way. A snail could have reached me faster. The plan was to step on him, but the minute I picked up my foot to get ready, the dumb fly rose up and landed on my knee! Forgetting the book, I smashed my palm down hard on my jeans. I'm sure it hurt, but I was too horrified to care.

There on my favorite jeans was a mass of gross, slimy, sticky, black fly guts. On my red palm were some stray black legs, looking like they were trying to run away.

"Yuck," I said out loud, staring down at the two final resting places of the deceased. My throat almost closed with the dozen impatient-to-get-out coughs this scene provoked.

"Yuck," echoed all the kids sitting close enough to see. Clyde jumped up and handed me some paper towels he grabbed from the sink.

"You want me to wet them?" Now that his life was no longer in danger, he was totally in control.

I shook my head and began wiping off the fly's remains.

Clyde stood right next to me till I was done, handing me fresh paper towels and taking away the ones with crushed guts on them.

He didn't say another word. He didn't have to.

Through it all Mrs. Harris kept on talking about the moon or whatever. I guess she had decided just to completely ignore me.

For the third time that morning, I raised my hand.

"Can I go to the bathroom to wash my hands?"

Mrs. Harris nodded. I think at this point she probably would have said yes to just about anything I asked.

I couldn't wait to get out of the room. I leaned

against the wall in the corridor, grateful for the opportunity to finally relieve the awful pressure that builds whenever I hide my tics for too long. As I relaxed, it was as if a dam had burst. My body sizzled with the unreleased coughs and sniffs and head movements held captive all morning. I inhaled deeply and opened my eyes . . . just in time to see, up close and personal, how looking at me makes other people feel. A dozen five-year-olds from Ms. Sanders's kindergarten class were holding hands and walking silently toward me. I stood rooted to the spot, helplessly watching them gawk, as if I were a car accident they were driving past, a mixture of horror and morbid curiosity etched on their little faces.

5

I froze. The kind of noise sirens make when a leak is discovered in a nuclear power plant began sounding in my head. The little kids continued silently down the hall. I forced myself to move, walking quickly straight ahead until I was able to duck into the girls' bathroom.

Totally spent, I turned the cold water on full force and faced the mirror. It was a bit of a surprise to see plain old ordinary me, not some nine-eyed freak looking back. I shook my head to empty it of the picture of the quivering, squirming, gasping typhoon those poor five-year-olds had just witnessed. You would think, at this point, I might cry. Instead, I took out a useless lozenge and forced myself to focus on something pleasant, the drama club's upcoming production of *Fiddler on the Roof.*

This was the third year in a row that Clyde and I both had parts in the school play. The club met three times a week after school to rehearse for next month's performance. Everyone in the cast had a few different roles. I was one of the daughters, a dancer, and the understudy for the mother. Clyde had a much bigger part. He was Tevye, the father who got to sing all the best songs. Clyde also helped build the set and paint the scenery.

The director of the show, Ms. Anderson, is also the school psychologist. She is younger than most of the other teachers and very cool. She lives in New York City and drives a red sports car. She loves hip-hop dancing and wears the best beaded bracelets.

At the beginning of the year, she called me into her office to ask some questions about my Tourette. Was I sleeping all right? Were my grades okay? Was anyone giving me a hard time in school? Things like that. She was familiar with the names of the medicines I had tried and nodded sympathetically when I explained that I was better off without them. I seemed to be handling the whole thing amazingly well, she said, and if there was anything she could help me with, I should come by and let her earn her salary.

What's weird about Tourette is that it seems to leave the building whenever I get up on the stage. When the music starts, it's like a protective barrier that slides between my skin and my symptoms. You would think that with everybody staring at me, I'd be more scared, but it doesn't work that way. Oh, sure, sometimes I might feel a twinge, but it's never interfered with my performance. Clyde's the same way. I'll bet if a mosquito was flying around onstage and we were in the middle of a scene, he wouldn't even see it.

I memorized my part and almost everybody else's. In fact, that's what I was forcing myself to think about now . . . my lines.

I heard the bathroom door open. I raced into a stall and closed the door. Although my heart was beginning to return to normal, I wasn't quite ready to see anyone yet.

The bathroom was quiet. I didn't move. Neither did whoever walked in. After a minute, a soft voice asked, "Carrie, are you all right?"

It was Ms. Anderson.

"Yeah, why?" I answered through the door.

"Well, Ms. Sanders just buzzed me to say she saw you in the hall and you seemed upset."

How kind.

I could hear Ms. Anderson breathing right outside my door. Slowly I opened the door and looked her right in the eye.

"I just had one of the worst mornings of my life. Our substitute teacher thinks I'm a nutcase. I saved Clyde from a major anxiety attack by killing a humungous, disgusting fly with my bare hands. I probably gave twelve five-year-olds nightmares. And it's not even lunchtime." I stopped to take a breath.

"Oh, in that case, Ms. Sanders must have been mistaken," Ms. Anderson said with a small smile. She put her arm around me and squeezed.

"Really," she said seriously, "coming in to talk to me doesn't mean you're not doing a great job with everything on your plate. Why don't you and Clyde think about joining the Lunch Bunch? I think both of you might find it helpful."

All I knew about the Lunch Bunch was that it met in Ms. Anderson's office at noon each day. Being part of the group isn't embarrassing like help class or detention, where everyone knows where you're going and why. Actually, the whole thing is sort of mysterious and private. It's strictly voluntary, so kids are there because they want to be, not as a punishment for bad behavior or a cure for a poor score on the standardized reading test. I know one kid who joined right after his parents divorced. Another girl I know went for a few months when her little sister was in the hospital with leukemia. Jesyca was in the group, maybe to increase the wattage of her dim bulb. I just assumed Lunch Bunch was for kids with problems they couldn't handle. I was doing fine handling mine. Ms. Anderson had even said so.

"I don't think so, but thanks for asking," I said shortly, brushing past her toward the bathroom door.

"Sure," she said softly as she folded her arms and leaned back against the bathroom sink. "If you and Clyde ever just want to stop by and see what's going on, that might not be a bad idea."

There was something in the kind way she spoke—

or maybe it was the way she seemed to look straight inside me—that made me nervous. Why was she making herself comfortable when it was obvious I was racing toward the door? As if she knew something about me I didn't know. It occurred to me that this scared feeling must be familiar to Clyde. Suddenly I had to get out of there. I turned away and tried to hide my sniffing behind a paper towel I grabbed from the dispenser on the wall.

"I better get back to my class," I called out, stumbling into the hallway. It was an almost impossible feat but somehow I managed to leave the bathroom in worse shape than when I went in.

"Carrie, I have to tell you something," Clyde murmured, speaking in that way he has of not moving his lips.

We were sitting in the rear of the auditorium after school, watching Ms. Anderson run through one of the show's production numbers. It was dark back there and far enough away from the rest of the cast for my tics not to bother anyone.

"Why do you have to act like we're being taped?" I asked, running my hand back and forth over the armrest. "No offense, but look around. Nobody but me cares about what you're going to say."

It was true. There was no one remotely within listening distance.

Clyde ignored me and plowed ahead.

"You know yesterday, when I left school early?"

"Don't tell me you have to go back to the dentist again." I was trying to be sympathetic. Sometimes it's hard, though. As if Clyde didn't have enough problems, he had an overcrowded mouth. He'd explained that that meant he had too many teeth jam-packed together. Twice already he'd had to have a few teeth pulled. Yesterday he had gone for a checkup.

"No. Worse." He exhaled loudly and put his feet up on the back of the seat in front of him. That was a big deal for Clyde. It was almost breaking a rule.

Now he had my attention. To me there are very few things worse than a dentist yanking the teeth out of your mouth.

"I was walking home, kind of slow 'cause I wasn't in a rush to see Dr. Kronish, when all of a sudden I saw it." Clyde's voice broke. "Ohmigod, Carrie, it was so scary." Clyde's legs came crashing down to the floor and he leaned forward. His eyes grew large, like someone was chasing him that very minute.

I felt a prickly sensation under my skin.

"On the corner of Lincoln and Bromley, I saw this pigeon. He was sitting on the sidewalk, near the curb, like he was waiting for a bus or something. As I got near him, I expected him to waddle away, but he couldn't care less that I was coming closer. It was like he was thinking of something important and didn't notice me. But it didn't make sense. Birds always move out of the way."

I sat back and started to relax. How bad could a bird story be?

"Then I stood right over him." Clyde gulped. "I reached my foot out to test him, to make him move. But he just fell over." He paused for a second. Then he hissed, "Stiff from rigor mortis." Clyde put his hands over his eyes and shook his head. "He was dead as a doornail."

My first thought was that I was proud of Clyde for getting that close. He was so paranoid with these birds and the mosquito thing.

"Wow." I shuddered. "You must have freaked." I was glad I hadn't been there because, to be honest, if I had seen this pigeon topple over like some baby toy, I might have puked.

"Not really," Clyde continued. "I knew from Sunday's paper that he looked exactly like the picture of one of the dead birds who were infected with the West Nile virus. I was sure the health department would want to see him, so I ran home and got a pair of my mother's tongs and a shopping bag."

"Whoa," I cried, "don't tell me you—"

"Well, I couldn't just leave him there for the mosquitoes to munch on."

I felt my mouth dropping.

"Carrie, I picked him up," Clyde groaned. "He was staring right up at me."

Goose bumps traveled up and down my arms.

"Then I slid him into this big Victoria's Secret shopping bag we had in the closet. I left him on the back porch and looked up the number of the health department."

"You called the health department?" I was impressed. Ordinarily I'm the braver one, but no way would I be dealing with a stiff, wide-eyed dead bird on my back porch.

"Well, the newspaper said they track these birds and if the mosquitoes around here got to him first, we all might be in trouble." Clyde leaned forward and got right in my face. "The bird was two blocks from here. One block from your house. Around the corner from mine. He could have fed dozens of mosquitoes." He leaned back in his seat, exhausted from reliving his adventure.

"All right," I put in, "what did the health department say?"

"You're not going to believe it. No one cared. I couldn't get anyone interested, even a little bit. Each person kept saying, 'Hold on, we'll connect you with the right person,' and I got bounced from one extension to the next."

"So then what?"

"Then nothing. I had to go to the dentist."

"So where's the bird now?"

"Well, that's what I wanted to ask you. Will you come over after school and help me bury him? It said in the paper they should be buried three feet deep."

This story was getting worse and worse.

"Why don't you ask your parents to help you?" I asked desperately. "I'm sure they wouldn't expect you to do it all by yourself."

"I haven't told them," Clyde said quietly. "If I did, they'd be annoyed that I made a big deal out of nothing."

I had to admit I knew how they felt.

"If I told my family, they would say the same thing they always do, that I shouldn't worry. That there's no danger. As if I had a choice about how worried I am. My father would probably defend the health department and say they've tested enough birds by now. As if that's the point." Clyde's voice rose. "I'm not crazy, Carrie. No one cares."

"Okay, take it easy," I said soothingly. "I think you were extremely brave. You might have even saved some people's lives."

I really didn't believe the last part, but he certainly deserved some words of praise for what he'd done.

"So you'll help me?"

"Yeah. I'll help you."

My shoulder felt stiff. I rotated it, my newest tic, until I heard it crack. Then I did it again. For a few moments we sat there, the two of us, listening to my shoulder make cracking sounds. It was my body's way of announcing to the world that I was getting tense. Not that, in this case, anyone could blame me.

"I'll help you get rid of the bird," I whispered, "if you promise to try to chill a little over this mosquito thing."

"Can you promise to stop sniffing? Did I ever once ask you to quit shrugging your shoulder? It's the same thing. I hate feeling this way as much as you hate your tics. We both can't help it."

That shut me up.

"And I'm telling you now," Clyde went on, encouraged by my silence, "I'm not going out at lunchtime anymore. No matter what. I'll hide in the closet or the bathroom or something. I'm not going to stand out there in the schoolyard for a half hour waiting to have my brain attacked. I won't."

"Okay, Okay, we'll figure something out." I sighed.

The only way I could keep him inside every day at lunchtime was to suggest we spend it with Ms. Anderson and her group of oddballs.

I should talk about oddballs, right?

7

It was five o'clock by the time the rehearsal ended. As I walked home with Clyde, I tried to think of all the things I could be doing that would be worse than digging a grave for a dead bird in a Victoria's Sc cret shopping bag. It was a very short list.

"I'll get the shovel out of the garage. You get the bag from under the table on the back porch and meet me in front of the tree by the fence," Clyde instructed.

I couldn't remember the last time I'd taken orders from Clyde. Hesitantly I walked around the side of the house to the back where the table was. I squatted down and my eyes narrowed. I squint during the scary parts in movies. I squint when I hear my parents fighting with Clementine. And man, was I squinting now.

The bag couldn't have been any pinker. Or have had any more hearts on it. If I grabbed it by the handles and didn't look inside, I might survive. I held my breath and picked it up. It was heavier than I'd imagined. I held it away from my body and walked back to the tree. Clyde was already digging.

He looked up at me and laughed.

"How sick is it that you're not at all grossed out when this thing is flying around full of a deadly virus, but now that it can't hurt you, you're petrified?"

I would have been stupid to deny it. I hated being near that bird. This had to be one of those boy-girl things. Every girl I know would agree it's just plain creepy to be near dead things.

"Stop talking and dig," I ordered. "Can I put this down?"

Before Clyde could answer, I gingerly placed the bag on the grass. Immediately it tipped over. The pigeon slid to the top of the bag and his head peered out. He was lying on his side. One eye stared up dully.

I covered my mouth and moved backward.

Clyde continued scooping out a hollow in the dirt.

"You don't look so good," he said, glancing up at my pale face. "You're not going to barf, are you?"

I didn't answer because I wasn't really sure. I looked up at the sky and took a deep breath.

"If you think you might hurl, aim it in this hole."

He seemed almost cheery.

After what seemed like an hour, Clyde pulled out his mother's folding wooden yardstick, which was in his back pocket.

I should have known if the newspaper said bury the birds three feet deep, Clyde would make sure he obeyed.

"Let me dig a little," I said, snatching the shovel from his hands.

I made the hole a little wider to accommodate the bag, whose contents refused to be bent or folded in any way.

"I think that's big enough," Clyde said. He picked up the bag by the handles and I heard a thud as the bird fell to the bottom of the bag.

I took another deep breath and watched as Victoria and her secret disappeared in the dirt. Clyde quickly refilled the hole.

"Thanks, Carrie, really," he said as I walked him back to the garage. "I couldn't have done it without you."

"What're you talking about? You did everything yourself. All I did was supply the nausea."

"That's not true," Clyde said. "It was so easy with you here. I wasn't nervous. I didn't keep thinking that my parents were going to come home any minute. I wasn't checking for mosquitoes. You helped, believe me."

I smiled on my way home, thinking how strange life is. Who would have thought that during that whole stressful time, I wouldn't tic once?

• • •

Two nights later I sat at dinner with the permission slip for joining the Lunch Bunch in my pocket. Ms. Anderson had seemed really happy about Clyde and me signing up. I'd sort of said I was coming with Clyde . . . that he really needed to be in the group but wouldn't sign up unless I went with him. It was at least 98 percent true.

What was 100 percent true was that although Clyde had heard the name Lunch Bunch, he, like most of the kids in school, hadn't a clue what went on there. He didn't really care, as long as it was inside. He would have joined the needlepoint society or the paint-scraping club, anything in a mosquito-proof environment. I heard they did all kinds of exercises, like imagining yourself in different relaxing places and playing word games that were supposed to make you feel better about yourself. If we didn't want to participate, we didn't have to, Ms. Anderson said, but she was sure we would want to.

Needing to have a permission slip signed was an unexpected bump in the road. I was sure my parents would blow this all out of proportion. If they sensed I was joining for any kind of psychological reason, they would drive me crazy. "Why do you need the psychologist? What are you going to talk about? Is anyone bothering you? Are your grades suffering?" And of course, "How come you didn't come to us if you have a problem?"

My mom is like a 1950s mom from the black-and-white sitcoms on Nickelodeon. You know, the ones wearing an apron and high heels all the time, smiling through whatever calamity takes place. She is great at making nice and cleaning boo-boos. My father, on the other hand, is right out of one of those reality-based police documentaries where the cops may be scared or confused or worried, but they'll never show it. Heroes, they deal easily with difficult problems that have quick, cut-and-dried solutions. Unfortunately, my dilemma is ongoing, a complicated one that needs more than a Band-Aid and less than a shoot-out.

God, how I wished they didn't have to know.

I decided to ask Clementine the best way to approach them. She gets them to say yes in twelve seconds to just about everything. I knocked on her closed door. In the past week she'd added three more names to her list of heroes who didn't graduate from college: Peter Jennings, Steven Spielberg, and the Dalai Lama.

"Come on in!" She yelled as if I were a half mile away. She does odd things like that all the time. She was sitting at her computer, gazing at her screen saver, which read GOOD ENOUGH NEVER IS. The walls were intensely blue and covered with shelves crowded with collections of plastic ponies from when she was in elementary school, floating candles, inflatable picture frames, and a cheerleader Barbie doing a split. Clementine sat on an inflatable chair near an old lamp she had painted blue and trimmed with a feather boa.

"Welcome to my world," she said glumly.

"Is this a bad time?" I asked anxiously. "I need your advice on something, but I could come back. . . ."

Clementine believes that in one of her previous lives she was a mighty king, because she so likes making people do what she tells them. It looked like she had come across someone who disagreed with her today. Though what amazes me is how infrequently that happens.

To my sister, it's like the rules of the world were made for other people. She runs out of the house every morning with a wet head and never gets sick. When she wore braces, instead of getting the invisible kind, she got the shiniest ones and then made sure she asked for the weirdest-color rubber bands so everybody saw them.

"Oh, please," she sighed dramatically. "Your problem is just going to wait until it's a good time for me? I don't think so. Unsolved problems fester; they get worse if you don't address them. What's up?"

I told her the whole story about the mosquito and the dead bird, the incident in the hall, and Ms. Anderson.

"I just want Mom and Dad to sign the stupid form without making a big production out of it. I'm only going so Clyde will have a place to be at lunchtime. He'll never go by himself."

"Well," answered Clementine thoughtfully, "they're not going to buy that. They're going to try to convince you that you don't belong in a group with kids talking about their problems."

That wasn't helpful.

"It's time you were honest with them. Mention Clyde, but don't make him the reason you want to join."

"What do you mean?"

"He's not the reason, Carrie. Face it. Mom and Dad are no help at all with this Tourette thing, pretending that everything is normal. They think if they ignore your tics, you'll forget you have them or no one will see them, or something stupid like that. They're afraid if you start talking about your Tourette and how you feel about it with other people, they'll have to start talking about how they feel about it with you. And they don't know what the heck to say."

This was not the conversation I wanted to be having. I started to crack my shoulder. Clementine winced.

"Does that hurt?"

"Only after about the twentieth time," I answered matter-of-factly.

Her sympathetic look triggered a brilliant thought.

"Hey," I said, "what about you signing the permission slip? You can even sign your own name—just use a 'C' instead of your whole first name. It's hardly a crime at all. Ms. Anderson is not going to check, because why would anyone want to forge a note to get into a group like this?"

Clementine hesitated. As strange as her behavior is, she's probably a more honest person than I am.

"Listen," I continued, "you said yourself I needed

to talk about this stuff. What if Mom and Dad refuse to sign it? Then I'll be left cracking both shoulders because I'll be spending lunch hour hiding in a closet with Clyde."

Clementine smiled.

"I couldn't bear to have that on my conscience." She got up from her chair and walked over to give me a hug. "Don't think I'm ever going to do this again," she said, trying to be stern. "Give me the note and let's never discuss this ever took place."

I fumbled through my book bag and handed her the folded paper. She opened it, scanned the description of the Lunch Bunch, and reached for a pen.

"Not orange ink, okay?" I pleaded.

"Well, I don't own anything that writes black or blue." She shrugged.

"Here," I said, handing her one of my pens. "Keep it."

She signed the permission slip—C. Peller—with her most adult-looking signature.

"Thanks anyway," she replied, handing me back my pen. "But what could I say with a pen that writes in blue?"

8

At lunchtime the following Monday, Clyde and I walked down the hallway to Ms. Anderson's room. When I'm nervous, I don't talk. Clyde, on the other hand, can't shut up.

"So you said you could just sit there and not say anything, right? 'Cause I'm not about to tell a bunch of losers that I'm crazy."

For the umpteenth time I told him he didn't have to participate if he didn't feel like it. His whining like a hungry cat was really getting annoying. Here I was, being the world's best friend, going along with him and putting myself in a situation where I was definitely going to tic. And probably have to talk about it.

Whenever I'm introduced to people I don't know, Tourette becomes my middle name. I hate it.

"So tell me again, what do they do there?"

"Shut up, Clyde, I'm done making you feel better. You're going to be fine in there. There are no mosquitoes in room twenty-seven. Look, I never promised it was going to be fun, but it beats the schoolyard, doesn't it?"

He was quiet the rest of the way.

My legs felt like spaghetti as we approached Ms. Anderson's office. As if she had X-ray eyes, she opened the door just as we got there.

"Come on in," she said warmly. "We were just waiting for the pizza deliveryman. Find a seat in the circle. Everyone, you know the drill. Introduce yourself to Carrie and Clyde."

Five kids sat on a round yellow rug in the center of Ms. Anderson's small office.

"I'll start," said one of the boys. "I'm Tim and I'm in eighth grade. I play tennis and I love Britney Spears."

They all laughed together, keeping us both outside.

Tim bulged everywhere . . . his cheeks, his chin, his stomach—even his sneakers had a pudgy look to them. Imagining him on the tennis court took my mind off how fast my heart was beating.

"Hi, guys, you already know I'm Jesyca."

Oh, did we ever.

Jesyca drew her legs up and wrapped her arms around them. I noted that today her lip gloss matched her Pepto-Bismol–colored fingernails.

"I collect Susan B. Anthony dollars and autographs of famous people, and I take piano lessons. My favorite store is Abercrombie and Fitch."

I wished Clementine were here. She'd have the best funny stuff to say about Jesyca.

"My mother spelled my name J-E-S-Y-C-A so I'd at least have one original thing about me." She looked around as if expecting applause.

IQ must be genetic, I thought.

"Hey, how ya doing? I'm Evan. I play basketball, worship Adam Sandler, and beat everyone I've ever played at Game Boy."

A little snotty, I thought. And hard to believe. Evan spoke so slowly, like he was a beat slower than the rest of the world. Did you ever have the radio and television on the same station? The radio is on a seven-second delay. That's what Evan sounded like.

I glanced over at Clyde. He was sitting with his hands around his ankles. His face was almost hidden behind his knees. When he saw me, the corner of his mouth turned up slightly. No one else would ever see it but me. In that teeny movement I knew not only that he understood what I was feeling, but also that he felt the same way. That's why, pain that he is, Clyde is my best friend.

"Hi, I'm Rebecca," said this really pretty girl with long dark hair.

She looked right at me and smiled. I felt myself smiling back.

Rebecca obviously didn't recognize me. That was a little strange. We'd been in the same jazz class on Tuesdays after school since September. None of the twelve of us in the class were friends, but I couldn't believe I didn't even look familiar to her. At least that proved that along with being onstage in the play, the dance studio was the other blessed tic-free zone in my world. Otherwise, she'd have remembered me, all right.

"I remember how scared I was the first time I walked into this room," she said, talking directly to me as if there were no one else in the room. "It's so hard because you don't know what to expect. Just know we're no different from anybody else in this school, except if we have a problem, we deal with it."

Rebecca shoved a shiny hank of hair behind her ear. There was something about her I liked. Maybe it was the confidence behind her words. Or the fact that she was a really good dancer who came to class like I did to work hard and master the routine. Or maybe it was the way she fixed her eyes directly on me. I nodded, just a tiny move, to let her know I got the message.

Next this really tall kid named Jon spoke. Clyde and I know him as the supersmart geeky kid in charge of the lighting for the play. Although I had been in the same place with him a million times, I don't think we had ever said hello. In fact, I don't think I had ever seen his eyes before. He's always looking down.

"I collect baseball cards, shark teeth, and mini cars," he began. "I love macaroni and cheese, and Pop-Tarts, and I drink a quart of Gatorade every day."

It looked to me that he had grown so fast, he didn't know where his body was. His mouth was pinched in this mean expression, but when our eyes met, I saw it was more because he was so uncomfortable having to talk than that he was really nasty. I couldn't decide why he didn't acknowledge that he knew who we were. Either he was ridiculously shy or in such a world of his own that he actually didn't recognize us. No matter, he was one odd duck regardless of the reason.

"Very nice," bubbled Ms. Anderson. "It's not easy to decide how to introduce yourself to someone new. Good job, everyone." Then she put the recently arrived box of pizza in the center of the circle and plopped down next to me.

"Okay, guys, it's your turn," she ordered, raising her chin slightly toward Clyde.

Clyde took a deep breath. I wished he were facing me now so I could flash him an encouraging look.

"My name is Clyde and I'm in seventh grade. I have the lead part in the school play, a baby brother named Emmett, and last week Carrie and I buried a dead pigeon who might have had the West Nile virus in my backyard."

I wanted to kill him. Suddenly my shoulder needed to be cracked so badly.

The group was silent. To their credit, no one smirked or rolled their eyes.

"I'm Carrie and I'm here mainly to keep Clyde company." This was how I'd planned to begin, before it got to be my turn. Before I knew that my head would choose this minute to snap toward my shoulder three times in a row.

Everyone sat very still.

"I'm also in *Fiddler on the Roof.*" I had to pause because my unsuccessful attempt to stop my head from jerking had all my attention. "The most fun thing I do is take jazz dancing, and the reason my head is doing that is because I have this disorder called Tourette Syndrome." The last sentence came out in a rush. Then I cracked my shoulder. Loudly.

The room was quiet for what felt like a very long time.

Then Rebecca said, "I'm starving."

Ms. Anderson opened the box of pizza and everybody started talking.

I felt like my spine had collapsed. I didn't even want to look in Clyde's direction. Even if he said I didn't sound bad and no one was freaked out, I wouldn't believe him.

"Hungry?" Rebecca crawled back from the middle of the circle to the space Ms. Anderson had sat in before she got up to pour drinks. She was very carefully dragging two plates. She put one in front of me. "The pizza from Attilio's is the best," she said as she took a big bite out of her piece. "Free food is another bonus for joining us."

I saw Ms. Anderson watching us.

"I'm sure it is," I mumbled, avoiding her eyes, "but I don't think I can eat anything right now."

"Why, because of your head thing?" Rebecca took another gigantic bite out of her pizza.

"Yeah, because of my head thing," I snapped. "You didn't see that kid Evan stare at me. It's humiliating in the middle of introducing yourself to have your head—"

"Decide to boogie?" Rebecca interrupted.

That stopped me cold. I never would have thought to describe my head jerking that way.

"Evan smells like dirty socks." She shrugged, gulping down her Coke. "You couldn't very well introduce yourself and not tell us about Tourette, could you?"

I couldn't believe someone I'd just met was talking to me this way.

"Besides, we all have our reasons for eating lunch in this room. You're ahead of the game. Everybody knows yours already. Now they have to tell you theirs." She smiled again and touched my shoulder. "The rest is a piece of cake."

I felt her hand on my shoulder long after she took it away.

A half hour before, I would have repeated that the only reason I was there was to help Clyde. Now that would make no sense. In a way, what I had planned to say was more embarrassing than the fact that I'd showed them my tics. What was I trying to do, pretend I was better than they were?

I looked across the room and saw that Ms. Anderson was taking this all in. I would have thought she'd be smiling, seeing how Rebecca was being so nice to me. But instead her expression was serious, like she was trying to figure something out.

9

Making a new friend is a lot like buying new sneakers. Although dozens are the right size, very few are really comfortable. It's hard to describe exactly why the one you choose fits. It's like a Goldilocks thing . . . you're the only one who can tell when it's just right. You sort of mold into each other, until after a while, it feels like you've had them forever.

Rebecca is like that. She transferred to the middle school at the beginning of the year from Manhattan. She lives with her mother, her mother's soon-to-be-fourth husband, two half sisters, a half brother, and a dog named Wiley, who, she made clear, was her favorite family member.

"I hope I didn't weird you out today," Rebecca said

when she phoned that night. "I'm sorry if I came on too strong, but I've been the new kid in these kinds of groups so many times, I knew exactly how you felt. This is my ninth school since kindergarten. Guidance counselors always figure I've got to be screwed up from all the moves, so they automatically slide me into whatever counseling group is running."

We'd been on the phone for about five minutes and I hadn't a chance to say a word beyond hello. Which was actually a good thing. It was taking a while to get over the idea that Rebecca had just looked up my number and called.

"You're thinking, 'I've got enough problems. No way am I going to open up to this bunch of mental cases,' right?"

That was exactly what I thought.

"By the way," she went on, "you do watch *The Simpsons,* don't you?"

"God, you're good," I laughed. "I love that show."

"Me too," she said delightedly. "I knew it the moment I saw you—"

This time I interrupted her. "That I liked *The Simpsons?"* I joked.

"No," she said, "that we'd be friends."

I was silent. This was the second time in one day she'd had this powerful effect on me.

"Do you know that we're in the same dance class?" I blurted out.

"No way!" Rebecca exclaimed. "I'm so embarrassed. Please don't feel bad. When I get to dance class, I zone out. I sweat like crazy and forget about everything."

I knew exactly what she meant. There's something about the music, about learning the choreography and sharpening each move that leaves the problems of the world outside.

"That's okay. Anyway, thank you for today," I said, finally relaxed enough to sit down on my bed. "So where do you live?"

"In Sandsview," Rebecca replied. "Simple Simon, he's my mother's boyfriend, was bouncing around in this huge house after his wife ran away with their landscaper and left him with his kid. He can't even boil himself a cup of hot water for tea, let alone take care of a five-year-old, so when he met my mother at the Christmas party she catered for his company and he found out she was an experienced mom, he fell in love."

My head was spinning. She spoke as if she were telling me about a TV show, not the soap-opera details of her real family life. I've never been there, but I know Sandsview is an exclusive gated community on the beach in Port Washington. The houses all have swimming pools and tennis courts.

"Is your mother going to marry him?"

It was hard to tell how she really felt about her living situation.

"God, I hope not," Rebecca said as if I had asked her whether it was going to rain tomorrow. "He's an idiot and she has to slow down a bit between husbands, don't you think? Wiley and I need a rest before we morph with any more stepsiblings."

I marveled at how sophisticated and worldly she

sounded. I've never met anyone my age remotely like her.

"Besides, Simple Simon has his own little plane. To me, anybody who has a private plane has something to hide."

Suddenly my life seemed very black and white compared to Rebecca's. She lives hers on a giant IMAX screen.

"So are you busy this Saturday?" she continued without taking a breath. "I remember you said you play tennis and there's a court out back that no one ever uses."

We had done this exercise with Ms. Anderson that afternoon. It was called "I am a person who . . ." and you had to finish the sentence ten different ways. One of my sentences was "I am a person who plays tennis pretty well."

"I'm not sure," I said. "I sort of had plans to go to the movies with Clyde."

"Oh, right, Clyde." Rebecca hesitated for a second. Then she said with a laugh, "I'd ask him over too but there might be some mosquitoes flying around out here."

Clyde had finished five of his "I am a person who . . ." sentences with different reasons why he was afraid of mosquitoes. I was proud that he had the courage to admit how upset all the newspaper accounts made him, but as I heard Rebecca say it, I could see how she could think he was completely insane.

"Clyde and I have been friends since we were four years old," I explained. "He's always been frightened of strange things. But after so long he's almost like my brother. . . ."

"A half one, I hope," Rebecca interjected. "You don't want to share any of his crazy genes."

It wasn't really that funny, but I laughed. I was feeling so good, I hardly felt guilty that we were laughing about Clyde.

"If he's really like your brother, then he won't mind if you tell him you can't make it just this once, will he?"

Even though her tone was sweet and she was asking a question, it sounded like I didn't have much of a choice. I felt uncomfortable and flattered at the same time.

"Nah," I lied. "He won't care."

"Great. I'll tell my mother you're coming. She'll make us a special lunch."

"Thanks for calling . . . and for asking me over," I said before hanging up.

What I couldn't say, because I didn't want to scare her, was that her call made me feel beyond happy. That after just this conversation, I realized how much I missed having a girlfriend to talk to about dancing and underarm hair and *Teen People.*

I hung up and immediately called Clyde. As I waited for him to pick up, my neck started to ache. All that shoulder cracking often left me sore at night. It was funny that when I was talking to Rebecca, nothing hurt.

"Hey, what's up?" Clyde said. I had already talked to him once since we'd left school, to get the homework I hadn't had a chance to finish copying from the chalkboard.

"That girl Rebecca just called me," I blurted out. "She wants me to spend Saturday afternoon at her house."

"Yeah, so?"

"So we have plans to go to the movies Saturday."

"Yeah, and?"

He wasn't making this easy.

"And if it's all right with you, I think I'd like to go over to her house."

"You don't need my permission, Carrie," Clyde said coolly. "It's a free country."

"I know that," I snapped. "I'm not asking permission. We had plans, so I was checking to see if you minded if—"

"If you already told her yes, then what difference does it make if I say I mind?"

"Eat snot and die."

"Ooh, good one," Clyde answered sarcastically. "Have fun with Rebecca."

"Please don't be mad," I pleaded. "I think it was really nice of her to call me. She's so interesting. She lives in Sandsview and has a lot of stepbrothers and -sisters. You'd like her too."

"Not as much as you do, that's for sure."

"You know what, Clyde? I hope in your dreams a monster mosquito bites off the tip of your nose. Good-bye," I said as I slammed down the phone.

Sometimes Clyde could be such a total loser. But if that was true, how come I felt like he had just won?

10

"So who is this new friend?" Dad asked as we pulled out of the driveway on Saturday morning to go to Rebecca's house. "That's some street she lives on."

I knew Rebecca's address would impress him. I couldn't tell him about the Lunch Bunch, so I told him she just moved into the neighborhood and that she is in my dance class. As I talked, I felt the two-minute warning my body gives before my tics start. I should have known. Car rides, commercials, waiting in line . . . all were my tics' favorite times to appear. This was going to be major. I wasn't sure which was worse, being in the car alone with Dad when they began or having them happen in front of Rebecca's family.

You would think that would be a no-brainer. My dad has seen me tic, heard my shoulder crack, and watched me sniff and cough and jerk my head a hundred times. You would think I'd be more comfortable ticcing in front of him. You would think.

The only way I know that my dad even notices my tics is by watching the muscles in his jaw. Right under the skin, a few inches from his ears, the muscles race back and forth, up and down. No other part of his face gives any indication that he notices what's going on. He acts as if nothing unusual is happening, no matter how loud my noises get or how bizarre my behavior becomes. I used to be sure he tried to ignore my disorderly conduct because he didn't want to hurt my feelings. But after almost a year, I'd changed my mind.

Just last Sunday I'd watched his jaw tighten when we sat in a restaurant and I couldn't stop clearing my throat. He got up in a hurry, before dessert, and left my mother to pay the check, muttering something about having to make a call on the cell phone in his car. I knew he'd be more comfortable if he could wear a T-shirt that read MY DAUGHTER'S NOT OBNOXIOUS, SHE HAS TOURETTE. Then at least the world would feel sorry for him. . . . Certainly they wouldn't blame my actions on his parenting.

He wasn't paying attention to me now because he was embarrassed, mad even, and he hadn't a clue what to do with me.

Two can play his game. I pretended I wasn't aware that my head appeared to be trying to break my shoulder in two and that even someone a block away could hear me furiously clearing my throat.

"Rebecca just moved here from Manhattan," I answered calmly between tics. "She and her half brothers and sisters are living in her mother's boyfriend's house."

I knew that information just added fuel to the fire. It's not that Dad is a saint or anything, but he has his own book of rules and inviting children to live in a house with a mother's boyfriend is not included. According to his address, though, this guy was extremely rich and that sort of took the sting out of it.

As we got closer to Rebecca's house, my tics got worse. That's part of the curse. If I made a list of the ten worst moments in the day for my symptoms to occur—when I have to meet someone new, when I'm taking a test, when I'm trying to impress someone—ten out of ten times that's when they'll pop up. I can't tell you how much I hate when that happens.

Now I had my father clearing his throat. He hadn't looked over in my direction once during the whole ride. What was his problem? He wasn't the one being introduced to a new friend's whole family in such a state. He didn't even have to get out of the car and be acknowledged as my father, if he didn't want to. As I watched his jaw twitch, I got really angry. I know my dad hates my having Tourette as much as I do. But he's the adult. He should know better than to think he's doing me a favor by making believe everything was normal. If I could have punched him, I would have.

"What's the boyfriend's last name?"

"I don't know. Simon something."

"Simon Trask? Does that sound familiar?" Dad's voice rose. He turned in my direction, forgetting for a second, then faced the road once more.

"Yeah, that might be him, why?" I said with a fake yawn. I loved finally having his attention and wanted to milk it as much as I could. I purposely cracked my shoulder three times in a row. I'm pretty sure that's the habit that drives him the craziest; at least it is if the speed of his jaw muscles is any indication.

"Simon Trask is the most successful criminal-defense attorney on Long Island. His name is always in the papers. I've watched him in court a few times. He's very good at what he does."

Rarely had I heard my father's voice so adoring.

"Does he know who you are? Should I mention your name?"

My father hesitated for a second. I felt my face flush when it hit me. He probably didn't want Simon Trask to know that he and twitchy me were related.

"Nah, I'm pretty sure he wouldn't recognize my name," my dad said weakly.

I stared him down, willing him with all my might to turn and face me. But he wouldn't.

I sniffed extra loudly. Then I just let my head go. We drove the rest of the way in silence.

There wasn't anything he could say that would be

worse than that silence. Even if he admitted my tics made him sick or scared him, I could have handled it better than this charade. If he asked, then I would have a chance to tell him I would do anything in the world to make my tics stop. I would explain that it's still me trapped in this body with a mind of its own. And then I could finally tell him how much I miss being as close as we used to be, before Tourette.

11

As we slowly made our way down Rebecca's block, my father stared openmouthed at the quarter-mile approach up the Trask driveway. This was more than a beautiful home; it was an estate. There was a huge sculpture on the lawn, the kind that belongs in front of a museum. Once you passed through the massive black gates, you could see the tennis courts, a basketball court, the pool area, a birdbath, and a small pond. The area to the left was full of wildflowers, like a meadow you would see in the movies.

"Wow," my dad said, "this guy practices the right kind of law."

The moment we swung around the circular entranceway, the front door opened. A bald guy in an orange tank top too small to fit over his belly walked out with a very skinny, very blond woman wearing a stretchy black T-shirt that ended about two inches before her jean shorts. From far away she looked like she could have been one of Clementine's friends, except none of them would be able to walk in the strappy hot-pink high, high heels that Rebecca's mother had on.

"Welcome. I'm Tammy Peters," she chirped with a big smile, sticking her head right into my side of the car. "You must be Sherry."

Startled to find her face barely an inch away from mine, I didn't even correct her. In that split second I could tell she smoked, had had bacon for breakfast, and must have had some kind of surgery that made her mouth look like it had been pumped up with helium. I swear her lips were the size of China.

"Thank you for inviting Carrie to come over," my father said smoothly, in one swoop being gracious and getting my right name in. "I'm Bob Peller," he continued, extending his hand.

"Oh, no problem. I'm relieved that Rebecca will be off my back today. At this age, don't you find them impossible?"

My dad did a pretty good job of hiding how shocked he was that this should be their first exchange . . . with me sitting in between them.

He was saved by the guy in the orange tank. He had unwrapped a cigar, dropping the cellophane on the ground where he stood. "I know you," he growled, pointing his chin at my father. "You're with Ullman,

Kreigler, and Datz." He bit off the tip of the cigar and spit it out on the grass.

"Yes, that's right," my father answered. I could see he was flattered that Mr. Trask knew who he was. "And your reputation makes yours a name I know as well," Dad went on. He was smiling too widely, like his upper lip was glued to the top of his gums.

"You're with a nice little firm," Mr. Trask said. "Me," he went on, puffing furiously on his cigar, "I like a good challenge."

Then he went on and on about how much he'd made on some business deal and what percentage of the settlement he'd earned from the trial, as if we were there to hear him brag about his greatness.

My father stiffened, but his smile still stuck. His knuckles tightened around the steering wheel. Suddenly I felt the pressure building. No matter how I tried, no way could I control what was about to happen. My head started twitching. That got Rebecca's mother to finally remove her head from the car. The next thing I did was stupid.

I swung open the car door and stepped out. Mr. Trask stopped talking, midbrag. He squinted and furrowed his brow, scoping me out without any tact at all. Most people look away or sneak a peek when they think I'm not looking, but not him. He watched me like I was a television show.

"Jeez, what's wrong with her?" he asked, directing his comments at my father. He chomped down extra hard on his cigar.

"You have to excuse Carrie," my dad replied dully.

"She has Tourette Syndrome. It's actually the most common unknown disorder. . . ." His voice trailed off.

I stood near the front bumper, in between Mr. Trask and my dad, not that Dad noticed. The sun prevented me from seeing inside the car.

"I defended a guy with that once," Mr. Trask went on, directing his remarks at my father. "He cursed something awful, right in the middle of his testimony. I'll never forget that," he added, shaking his head.

There's a game I play whenever my tics make me feel this crappy. It's called "What would I promise not to do ever again if only my head would quit?" I'd never eat another French fry. I'd never laugh at another Mike Myers movie. I'd never wear sneakers. But in real life the only thing guaranteed to help would be if I never breathed.

"I don't curse, don't worry," I told Mr. Trask. "This is usually as bad as it gets." I prayed that my father would jump in and rescue me, but he remained silent. "Anyway, where's Rebecca?" I said lightly, practicing one of the acting tips Ms. Anderson had taught us. I pretended I was a girl who didn't care that a horrible, rude man had just sucked all the confidence out of her body while her dad sat and begged him to excuse her disgusting behavior.

I made a move in Mr. Trask's direction. He jumped out of my way, as if my head twitching were contagious. Up close he looked pale and mushy, the kind of guy who probably thinks flossing is a form of exercise. His eyes widened as I got closer, revealing lots of blood vessels zigzagging over the white parts of his eyeballs. I wished I could stuff that fat cigar down his throat. Instead, I stopped when I got right next to him and smiled. I cracked my shoulder, loudly, on purpose. Then I walked toward the house.

I left without saying good-bye to my father, grateful for once to concentrate on not stepping on any cracks on the path. Rebecca's mom followed, rattling on about the rigatoni and broccoli she'd prepared for lunch. I couldn't decide if she was purposely ignoring what had just happened or if she had even been aware. It didn't make a difference.

Rebecca seemed really happy to see me. My head relaxed as soon as I saw her.

"Isn't my mom a space cadet?" she asked, laughing, as we walked to the tennis courts. "Don't worry about the belly-button ring. It's not real. She just wears it on the weekends when Simon is around." She shrugged. "I don't know how old he thinks my mom is, but whatever works."

I had been too humiliated to notice Mrs. Peters's belly button, but I hoped my dad had seen it. That would make him nuts.

The rest of the day was fun. We played tennis, fed the fish in the pond, and ate outside on a patio overlooking the bay. Not that I was surprised, but Rebecca's room was beautiful enough to be featured in a magazine. Everything looked like it had been picked out and put together yesterday, down to her collection of beach glass and "Got milk?" ads. There was a television, a CD player, and her own telephone with an answering machine. She had a computer and a printer. And she had her own bathroom filled with all the most expensive shampoos and soaps.

"So what did you think of My Way or the Highway Trask?" she asked as we plopped down on her bed with diet Cokes. "Don't even try to lie."

Just thinking about him woke up my tics. I started to clear my throat. How could I say he was the most awful person I had ever met? And how could Rebecca live under the same roof and act like he was just a minor annoyance?

"Simon can be summed up with one story," Rebecca continued, not waiting for a reply. "When he's somewhere that doesn't allow him to smoke those horrendous cigars, he smokes horrible cigarettes. The first time we met, he was taking us out to this fancy restaurant. I saw him put his cigarettes in his jacket pocket. My grandpa came over to baby-sit for my sister. He quit smoking years ago, but whenever my grandma's not around and he's with someone who still smokes, he always bums one. Well, he asked Simon for a cigarette and Simon pulled out a pack from his pocket with only one left. Of course my grandpa wouldn't take it.

"I knew that couldn't be. A half hour before, he had had a full pack. Since then, I've learned his trick. Every day he puts the same pack with just one cigarette left in his left pocket and his regular pack in his right pocket. That way if anyone asks him, he shows them the one cigarette. Anyone who is a smoker would never take someone's last cigarette." She paused to let the full impact of what a creep this guy was sink in. Then she added, "And he has millions of dollars, isn't that sick?"

12

"I have something special planned for today," Rebecca sang out the minute I walked though her front door the following Saturday. It was weird how we'd both just assumed I'd go visit again. Turns out I was as grateful to leave my house, where everyone hung around every Saturday morning, as Rebecca was for me to help fill the vast emptiness of her house. Everyone scattered early in Sandsview. Her mom took the kids to baseball practice and never reappeared before four o'clock. Simon played golf. It was even the maid's day off. So it was up to the two of us to find a way to enjoy the palatial Trask estate.

Clyde and I talked a little less every day. Clyde meant comfort and acceptance, but Rebecca meant freedom, excitement, and surprises, and who would turn that down? I watched as he noticed Rebecca and me wearing the same angel T-shirt and rubber bracelets. He never said a word but I knew it couldn't have made him feel very good. I never mentioned her name to him and we both pretended that everything was fine between us. Which, of course, now that we were keeping secrets from each other, it wasn't.

"Okay, now don't be mad at what I'm going to say," Rebecca began. "Sometimes friends tell you things you don't want to tell yourself."

It didn't sound like I was going to like what followed. I inhaled deeply and shrugged. "I promise I won't be mad."

"You definitely won't be mad," Rebecca chirped, "because as soon as I tell you what's wrong, I'm going to fix it."

"Fix what?" I sighed. This was taking entirely too long.

"All right. I'll give you a hint."

Then Rebecca got out a big bowl, a package of Kool-Aid, a small bottle of white vinegar, a few towels, and some sandwich-sized Baggies. She put everything out on the kitchen counter.

"Here's the deal," she said, suddenly all business. "I think you're really pretty, but the way you dress . . . your hair . . . you're kind of bland."

"Bland?"

"Yeah, you know, like the color beige. It's not a terrible color, but it's not too exciting, either. It's boringly safe. I think it's time for you to stop blending into the walls and add some color to your life. Try something new. Shake things up a little."

I looked at the Kool-Aid and Baggies and then at Rebecca's smiling face. Her cheeks were actually turning pink with excitement.

"What's that stuff for?"

"The first step of your makeover. You're going to walk out of here a new woman."

Just like that. Without allowing for the fact that it was *my* appearance she was about to change, she continued.

"Don't worry, it's not permanent. It'll wash out in a week or so."

"What will wash out?" I asked, trying to control the panic in my voice. Rebecca didn't seem to understand that maybe someone with completely unpredictable tics and jerks would rather blend into the walls than be the center of attention.

"Your hair, silly," Rebecca squealed. "I know the real you. The you that comes out when you dance. The you that could help you with the tic thing if you ever let it out."

The thought never occurred to her that I might object.

I didn't know what to say. I looked at the Kool-Aid to check out the color. Blue. I suddenly realized that although I was scared, deep down inside I loved the idea of seeing what I'd look like with blue streaks in my hair. Rebecca knew that about me before *I* knew that about me. She was already turning on the water in the sink and putting on these big yellow rubber gloves. When she noticed me standing there, not moving, she shut off the water.

"Carrie, please trust me about this. I would never do anything I wasn't positive would look great on you. I swear if you don't like it you can cut my hair yourself or color it with real dye or whatever. That's how sure I am that you're going to look amazing."

I looked at Rebecca, suddenly touched by all the trouble she'd gone through to get everything together. What was the worst that could happen? It would wash out, she'd said. Besides, I didn't know how to say no to her, anyway.

I started to unbutton my shirt.

"Do I have to take this off?"

"That would be smart," she agreed, immediately turning the water back on. "Just mix that package of Kool-Aid with a cup of hot water and a teaspoon of vinegar," she directed, walking over to the CD player set up on the kitchen table. Music blasted through the house.

I wet my head under the kitchen faucet. Rebecca carefully poured out a small amount of the color mixture into a Baggie and put a strand of hair into it. Then she closed the Baggie all the way up to my scalp and used a bobby pin to hold it in place. She repeated that about ten more times all over my head. When she was done, she wrapped my hair in a towel.

"Leave it in for an hour," she directed as she started cleaning blobs of blue from the counter and the sink. "Be careful not to get it on your hands or your face, 'cause we'll have to use nail polish remover to get it off."

Beyond exhilarated, I obeyed every word. While we waited, we danced around the kitchen and sang at the top of our lungs. This was completely new for me, impulsively taking a risk and making a decision without mauling it to death. It felt great.

After the hour was up, Rebecca told me to shampoo my hair. Then she brought down the dryer from her bathroom and made me sit on a stool near the breakfast nook, without a mirror in sight, while she blow-dried my hair.

After about five minutes she was done. I held my breath.

"Are you ready," she asked, "to see the real you?"

I jumped off the stool and ran to the mirror in the entranceway. It was perfect. My hair had fine, delicate streaks of blue that in the sunlight looked positively punk but in regular light were subtle enough to get by without causing a fuss. I couldn't wait to show Clementine.

"Oh, Rebecca, I love it!" I squealed.

"Stick with me, kid." She smiled, eyeing my rather beige outfit. "A trip to the mall is next."

I ran over and gave her a big hug. Immediately my neck stiffened as I realized she was just standing there. I backed away. Don't make a big deal over this, my brain screamed. Not everybody is the huggy type.

As if to prove my brain right, Rebecca said, "Come

here, I have a present for you." She opened a drawer near the sink and handed me a small box wrapped in shiny blue paper. Inside was a beautiful blue rhinestone barrette in the shape of a ballet slipper.

"What's all this for?" I asked.

"Duh, it's for your new hair."

I wasn't sure if she didn't understand what I was asking or chose to ignore it.

"It's beautiful. Thank you for everything."

But Rebecca was already on to the next activity. "Let's go show the sun your new look," she said, kicking off her flip-flops and slipping her feet into her sneakers. "The tennis court awaits."

It was a glorious day. It got even better when my thoroughly surprised parents told me they thought my hair looked good. "Cool," I think, was the word they used. In fact, everyone liked it or ignored it, except Clyde who said it looked like a giant blueberry had exploded on my head. I didn't care one bit.

13

A really good thing happened later that week. Mrs. Davis called me up to her desk one morning and asked if I wanted to be her attendance monitor.

"There's been a change in policy," she explained. "The school board wants a more accurate reporting of how many kids are in class every day and I'm in charge of tallying up the number absent from seventh grade. Would you be interested in going into the other four classes on the floor and picking up their attendance sheets? I don't care when during the day you decide to go as long as by three o'clock I have all four forms."

"Sure," I answered, already grateful for the excuse to leave the room whenever I needed to. I thought it a little strange that it took the school board until there were just six weeks left of school to put a new plan into effect, but who was I to question such rare good luck?

"Great," she said brightly. "I need someone I won't have to remind all the time, and I know you'll be on the case."

She was right about that. I never once forgot my job. For me, that break each day was a blessing. Picture yourself having to sneeze really badly. And you're in a place where everyone is sleeping. You can probably control it for a while. Maybe you can manage to postpone your sneeze for ten minutes. But sooner or later, that sneeze is going to come out. That's what it's like trying to hold in my tics. Now I had the perfect opportunity, on my way to the other classrooms, to duck into the bathroom and let them all out. I was more careful now, however—no more letting go in the hallways.

It also helped that I had a new friend. For most of the school year, after I got Tourette, it was easier spending time alone than feeling constantly embarrassed in front of Amy and Whitney. After a while I got used to it. Sometimes I felt a little bad about the way I'd just stopped being their friend without ever explaining why. But never bad enough to call them or make plans. I figured by this time they must have figured it out.

Rebecca was a different story. Although each of us had a load of crap to deal with, we hardly ever spent time complaining. She was the exact opposite of Clyde. I never worried about my tics with her; I discussed them endlessly with him. He's the kind of friend you could just lie on the bed and talk to for hours. She never stood still long enough to discuss anything more serious than how impossible it is to open a CD. When we were together, it was her mission to always come up with some fun thing to do. She was already busy planning a trip into the city to show me where we could buy fake Kate Spade bags.

• • •

Clyde came into the Lunch Bunch looking a little frantic. It wasn't like we weren't friends anymore . . . we still spoke about stuff, but things were definitely not the same. I tried to pretend that I was just as interested as I ever was in his mosquito madness, but he knew me too well. Even over the phone I knew he could sense that my toes were curling in my sneakers three minutes into the first recap of the six o'clock news.

The Saturday after my hair coloring, he called to tell me he was going with Jon from the Lunch Bunch to a Mets game. Jon's father worked for the team and could get tickets anytime. I was relieved he'd made other plans because I didn't know how to tell him Rebecca and I were going into Manhattan in Mr. Trask's limousine to walk around for a few hours while he took care of some work. Then he was taking us to Serendipity for lunch and their world-famous frozen hot chocolate.

I should have figured Clyde would be a wreck

that day. It had rained hard for two days, leaving puddles everywhere. I wanted to say something to make him feel better, but I didn't. Instead, I tried not to think about how he saw every clogged gutter filled with leftover rain as a maternity ward for millions of mosquitoes. In his mind, these babies were being born and bred for an all-out assault on everyone he loved.

Ms. Anderson picked up on Clyde's mood immediately.

"You know what," she said brightly, "today let's share one time when you were in a situation where things got so uncomfortable, you prayed that the earth would just open up and swallow you. A time when your face was red, your heart raced, your hands got cold and you felt—"

"Embarrassed?" interrupted Tim.

"Embarrassed times infinity," Ms. Anderson continued, ignoring Tim's outburst.

"I'll start; although to be honest, I have so many of those moments it's hard to choose one."

That's what's so nice about Ms. Anderson. She never acts like she's any different from us, just older, and always makes us feel she would have been sitting right here, in this room, when she was our age. Unlike a lot of other teachers, she never makes you feel that she's preaching something "for your own good."

"Okay, once, just before I graduated college," she began, leaning into the circle as if she were confiding a juicy secret, "we had to appear before a panel of three professors and give a three-minute speech on any topic we wanted. They were checking our voice and our diction, to make sure we sounded good enough to be understood by you guys." She inhaled deeply and shook her head as if to shake loose the humiliating memory.

"There were just two of us scheduled to speak. The other girl went first. After watching her carefully make her way up to the podium, I realized she was blind. Her speech was about how she wanted to work with blind children, how she wanted to show them they weren't limited by their disability."

Ms. Anderson sighed. "To be honest, I worried that my speech on how much I loved Broadway musicals was going to sound lame and make me look spoiled after hers. I started thinking about how she managed to get up to the fourth-floor office with no elevator. I wondered when she became blind . . . if it was an accident or an illness, if she had ever had her sight." She lowered her voice. We all leaned closer to hear.

"Then I realized I wasn't paying attention and she was finished. I popped out of my seat and raced to the front of the room." Ms. Anderson paused dramatically. "We collided a moment later. I knocked her down, flat on her back."

We all gasped. Talk about wanting to disappear through the floor.

"That wasn't the worst of it," she went on. "I picked her up, apologizing over and over, then took my place behind the podium. Then, instead of beginning my speech with its title, 'I'm a Broadway Baby,' I said, 'Birth Defects.' "

We sat silently.

"I guess it was on my mind whether she was blind at birth and the words just fell out of my mouth." Ms. Anderson closed her eyes and shuddered. "It was awful."

The room was quiet for a long moment; then everyone started to talk at once. One by one the stories came out.

"When I was six, I was the ring bearer at my sister's wedding," Evan began. "I was dressed in a tuxedo and I had to carry the rings on a pillow from the front of the church to the altar. While I walked down the aisle, everybody smiled at how cute I was. Then I farted, really loud. The whole place cracked up. My mother got so mad at me . . . like I did it on purpose."

The group laughed sympathetically.

Jesyca was next. She rolled her eyes, as if farting in front of everyone near and dear to you was no big thing. "Once last year, in sixth grade, I was walking in the halls and Scott Stoner was walking toward me." Scott Stoner was the most popular boy in school. He was handsome, got great grades, and was the best soccer player in the district. "He waved at me. I couldn't believe it. I didn't know what to do, so I waved back. Then he looked directly at me. In that split second I realized he wasn't waving to me, he was waving at his friends walking behind me." Jesyca put her hands over her eyes. "I was so humiliated."

Clyde and I made eye contact. Without saying a word we agreed she was an idiot of colossal proportions. This was a person who didn't know the meaning of humiliation.

"I once fell off the top riser in the chorus at the spring concert in front of a million people," offered Tim. "Everyone in the audience got scared. My mother ran up right onstage to make sure I was all right. And Mr. Kogan, the music teacher, was furious."

"Every time I tell a joke, no one ever laughs," Jon blurted out. "That's a horrible feeling. People just stare and I never know whether to apologize or disappear."

The group groaned.

"Your jokes are terrible, that's why," Evan said. "Where do you get them, off of Bazooka comics?"

"Okay, okay," Miss Anderson interjected. "This is not a time for sarcasm. Is that it?" she asked Jon kindly. "No one special horrifying story?"

Jon looked down at the floor. "I'm not sure I should share this story; it's a little gross."

"We love gross," Tim answered. "Come on, what?"

"Well, in fourth grade when I was a Cub Scout, we went camping overnight upstate. The scout leaders told us we had to rough it, you know, go squat behind a tree if we had to, you know. . . . I tried but I couldn't do that. I counted the hours till I'd be home to my own bathroom. The parents were supposed to meet the bus back at the school at five o'clock. The whole ride home I was busting. By the time we pulled up to the school, it was really bad. The school was locked, so I couldn't get in to use the bathroom. My parents were visiting my grandpa in Manhattan and got stuck in traffic." Jon's face turned red. He tried to smile. "In the fifteen minutes I wound up waiting in front of the school, you can guess what happened," he said in a whisper. "It was awful."

Tim made a stupid gagging noise. The rest of us told him to shut up.

"Rebecca, what about you?" Ms. Anderson asked.

I was praying it was half an hour into the future so this discussion would be over.

"Well," Rebecca started, "I have so many incidents to choose from. I could tell you about the night I came home from my father's house and saw my mother naked with her boss," she began, counting on her fingers. "Or the time when I was nine and I had to beg this cab to stop in the middle of the night to take my mother to the hospital to have my sister." She paused to gauge our reaction. When she saw she had our undivided attention, her voice got louder. "There was the day I walked up and down the halls of my new school in fourth grade and was fifteen minutes late in starting the standardized reading test because it was my fifth school that year and I couldn't remember the teacher's name or the room number."

Rebecca's eyes looked glassy, like she had a fever. I felt bad for her but suddenly a little scared of her too. The rest of the kids had had a hard time telling their embarrassing story. You could see it in how they spoke. That's the thing about the group. No matter what brought you into room 27, how different we all are, how little most of us have in common, it doesn't matter. All of us understand humiliation. And have experienced fear. And somehow feel better after sharing how we survived it all.

But Rebecca had such a hard edge, it was difficult to know how she really felt. "I could tell the story of when we were in a restaurant and my mother's third husband got into a drunken fight with the waiter and they threw us out . . . before dinner."

Ms. Anderson stood up. She was about to say something, but Rebecca wasn't finished. My stomach tightened.

"Or the time just a few weeks ago," Rebecca went on, "when the guy who owns the house we're living in, my mother's boyfriend, invited some friends over to watch a boxing match. It was eleven o'clock and I was already in bed, but he kept calling me to come down and get them some beer and snacks. I was wearing these ridiculous Powerpuff Girls pajamas. They all stopped talking and stared at me. I felt so stupid."

The group laughed nervously.

"You probably don't believe me"—she shrugged—"but those are just the first things that come to mind. If you gave me a few more minutes, I'm sure I'd have twenty more."

"That's okay, Rebecca," Ms. Anderson said softly. "I think we got the idea."

Rebecca never talked to me about any of those

times. Come to think of it, she never mentioned anyone . . . not a friend or a teacher, not even a neighbor . . . from her life before moving to Sandsview. Didn't she have anyone to talk to when these awful things happened? No wonder my tics didn't bother her.

The bell rang, saving Clyde and me from contributing. He gave me a small smile and a tiny thumbs-up sign. I smiled back.

For sure, Rebecca's stories were disturbing. But we both knew that if we ever told them *our* stories, we could blow them away.

14

"So how was school today?" my mother asked as she dished some string beans onto my plate. She settled back in her seat and looked straight at me. Her eyebrows raised, her smile already way too big, she waited for my reply. I felt sorry for her. She always expects to be entertained by some funny story and I never have one.

"No offense, Mom," I said, "but I hate when you ask me that question."

"Why?" she said, sincerely puzzled. "What's wrong with wanting to know how your day was? Would you rather I didn't care?"

Of course I'd rather she didn't care. I glanced

across to Clementine, but she was busy removing the small pieces of green pepper from her salad. Peppers were probably toxic this week.

"Nothing ever happens in school. You sign all my tests, so you know how I'm doing. It's the same old thing every day." I took a big bite of chicken to keep myself from going on.

I thought what would happen if every day I came home and told the truth. Oh, today Michael asked Mrs. Davis if he could change his seat because my noises were driving him crazy. Oh, today Clyde was acting weird because he's mad that I'm friends with Rebecca. Oh, today Rebecca invited me to go out to dinner with her family for her birthday on Saturday and I'm scared to go because her mother's boyfriend, Dad's idol, gives me the creeps.

I was doing her a favor by keeping quiet.

"Has the Tourette Syndrome been much of a problem?" my father asked, clearing his throat. "You seem to be handling it fine in school." He looked down, almost frowning, giving 110 percent of his attention to cutting his potato.

My mother's brows arched up; his knit together. It's funny how sometimes you hear more watching a person's face than listening to what they're saying. Body language, Ms. Anderson calls it. Well, the body language she taught us that indicates someone is interested in what you have to say . . . a welcoming smile, relaxed shoulders, direct eye contact . . . was not being practiced by my dad at this table. He asked a question and answered it with the words he wanted to hear. I felt tense, like my parents were already flinching from what I might share.

"The same," I said flatly. I wouldn't tell the truth, but I wasn't about to lie, either.

"Well, if Carrie's report card is any indication . . . ," my mother began, her voice trailing off when she noticed my expression.

"You have to keep in mind how lucky we are, Carrie, that your . . . problem hasn't affected your grades. Many children with Tourette have difficulty learning." She looked toward my father for support.

I hate when she says "we," like they have the slightest idea of what my life is like. Almost as much as I hate that she thinks I should feel lucky.

"Please, Mom," interrupted Clementine, rolling her eyes. "You're not about to launch into the 'how things can always be worse' spiel, are you?"

Although I agreed with her, I wished Clementine would keep quiet. I knew my mom was just clueless, not cruel, and hurting her feelings didn't improve my life at all.

Mom pursed her lips. Then she continued. "I always keep in mind that expression, 'I complained I had no shoes until I met a man who had no feet.' " She stared right at me. "We *are* lucky," she insisted.

I searched my brain for an escape from this conversation but couldn't think of anything to say. Instead, I started sniffing.

"Answer your mother." My father's voice assaulted me like a prison guard. He hated when I sniffed my food or the silverware.

"School was fine today," I said through gritted teeth. "We had a math test, I lent Jesyca a pen because hers ran out of ink, and rehearsals for the play are going to be every day after school starting next week." I sniffed loudly.

"Now, was that so hard?" my mother said without the teeniest idea how hard it had been.

Clementine winked. "I love when you share your experiences with us, Carrie," she said sarcastically. Then she did me the biggest favor and completely changed the subject. She started talking about the upcoming state regents' exams and how she needed money to buy some review books.

I thought about what had just happened. It isn't that I wanted to keep how miserable I was a secret. I just know my parents. They react to my Tourette the way they react when a neighbor's loud alarm starts blasting and no one turns it off right away. Mom never shows she even hears it; Dad prefers muttering under his breath, trying to hide his irritation. Neither one tries to solve the problem by checking on the house or calling the police.

My mind drifted to Saturday night. I loved that Rebecca chose me to celebrate her birthday with her. I was excited that we were going to this really fun restaurant in SoHo. I just dreaded being with Simon Trask.

I had to get up from the table before thinking about him caused me to start inhaling the silverware.

"May I be excused?" I asked quietly.

"Sure, honey." My mom smiled as if we had all enjoyed the most pleasant dinner.

Suddenly I felt really tired. As I passed her room, I noticed that Clementine had added Pablo Picasso, Mark Twain, and Marilyn Monroe to the list on her door. She is creative; I'll give her that.

When I reached my room, I closed the door behind me. There, in the dark, I let out what felt like a day's worth of unexpressed tics and shrugs and coughs. I caught a glimpse of myself in the mirror. I looked like a marionette that had a three-year-old controlling her strings.

The phone rang. It surprised me how much I hoped it was Clyde.

"Hey, what's up?" asked Rebecca.

"Not a lot," I answered. "I was just going to start my homework. How's your book report coming?"

Rebecca hated to read. It was surprising for such a smart girl, but she said she had trouble keeping her mind on the page, especially this time of year. All week she gave me a running page-count of how far along she was.

"I figured out a way to make it more bearable," she said. "Since I'm reading a paperback, I just rip out the pages as I read them. It makes me feel like I accomplished something and it gets lighter to carry each day."

This was not one of her best ideas, but I knew better than to say a word. Besides, it was none of my business. Rebecca gets away with doing things her way all the time. Why should she listen to me?

"That's cool," I lied, hoping to get off quickly and start my work. I just wasn't up to chitchat tonight. It sounded like someone was talking very loud in the background, although with so many kids around, someone was bound to be yelling.

"Oh, before I forget," Rebecca began, "I have something to tell you." She sounded weird, as if someone was standing right next to her. "Simon decided to invite his parents to dinner on Saturday night to meet us, so it's probably not a good idea for you to come along."

I didn't say a word.

"The next time we go, though, you'll come, definitely," she said in a rush. Then under her breath, she added, "It's not worth fighting about. He's a moron, don't feel bad."

She could have gotten away with me thinking this was a family get-together. I was ready to believe her. But Rebecca thought I could take the truth. Simon couldn't stand the idea of me sniffing and coughing through dinner in a fancy restaurant. I could imagine the conversation right before she called. Why couldn't Rebecca meet new friends on the soccer field or in dance class? What was her problem that she had to pick up a stray crazy from a group of troubled kids?

I debated asking her to tell me exactly what had happened but decided not to.

"No big deal," I answered instead, giving her what I hoped was my most nonchalant tone. "Another time." I sounded just like I imagined she would if the situation were reversed. Stiff upper lip or some such crap.

Enough already, I thought as I hung up. I began drumming my fingers on my desk. How many times in one hour could a person feel one way and have to act another?

15

You could almost smell that the end of the school year was approaching. Maybe it was the brightness of the sunlight, or the fact there were no more awful multiple-choice tests, or simply that everyone except Clyde wore shorts to school. Whatever the clue, the coming of summer is always good news.

Since Mrs. Davis had made me the attendance monitor, it was a lot easier to get through the school day. Every time I left the room, I stopped off to huddle in my favorite bathroom stall. In just a minute or two, it was over.

After a while it made no difference if there was someone in the stall next to me. I was just grateful for the chance to rotate my shoulder blades as if trying to make them meet in the middle of my back. I thrashed and shifted my lower jaw to either side and sniffed like a little rabbit. Then, completely spent, I released the lock and walked out, pretending that what had just happened was not the least bit peculiar.

It didn't hurt matters that the show was also going well. The time I spent onstage being someone else helped me pass for normal in real life. In those moments when the class looked at me and imagined I was like them—and inside I was hanging by my thumbs trying to hold in some odd behavior—I was grateful to Ms. Anderson and her acting tips.

Her advice during the Lunch Bunch was also helpful, even for frantic Clyde. Although he still wore long sleeves and pants to school and carried bug spray in his book bag, he seemed a little less on edge.

"You might consider the idea that there is more information about these mosquitoes than you're aware of," she said one day, handing Clyde some health department pamphlets about West Nile virus. "I'm an advocate of the belief 'Knowledge is power,' and right now I think your fears have more power than your brain has knowledge."

She waited for exactly the right moment to give Clyde that material. I watched as he folded the pamphlets in half and carefully stuck them in his back pocket. Had she offered them to him a few weeks ago, before he trusted her, they wouldn't have had the impact they did now.

"You want to hear something interesting?" he said the next day. Our class had let out a few minutes early and we were the first ones in the Lunch Bunch room. "Last night I read that mosquitoes usually fly around at about the same height as people. They don't fly high enough to bite people in high-rise buildings." I smiled, seeing how relieved Clyde looked just to imagine those times he would be high enough to feel completely safe.

"Did you see the part that says most of those who are bitten by the mosquito carrying West Nile virus don't get sick?" Ms. Anderson added, peering up from her desk. "And only one percent of those who do, die."

That's why she's great. Ms. Anderson treats your problem, whether it's with your parents, your friends, your teacher, your health, or in your head like Clyde's, with the utmost seriousness. At times she meets with each of us alone, but it never seems planned or forced. Whatever is discussed is confidential. She never makes you feel dumb, like the rest of the world does.

Clyde nodded. He had read that part, but it didn't bring him the same comfort as learning how high mosquitoes flew. That was a fact he could use to eliminate a danger factor.

"Did you see when they are most active?" Ms. A. pressed on. She understood what made him feel better. "The latest study out of Washington shows that the time to be on alert is between dusk and dawn."

I actually saw Clyde's shoulders fall.

"Really? Where did you read that?" he asked excitedly. If that was true, he could get through school a lot easier.

"I promise to bring in the study tomorrow." Ms. Anderson grinned.

I tried to return her smile. Although she also encourages me to read all I can about Tourette, the added knowledge doesn't work as well with me. I have never really understood the abnormal brain-chemistry thing. And finding out there are three to four times as many boys as girls with Tourette hasn't really lifted my spirits. Neither has learning that some symptoms last for a week, others a month, and still others might survive years.

Some of the research indicates that Tourette is inherited, but what can I do with that information? Blame my parents? All I really want is to be like everybody else. With all the drugs in the world, it's my luck that none can cure my sick brain. My best hope is that I will be one of the lucky ones whose symptoms lessen as they get older.

"Okay, now that we're all here, I'd like to begin," Ms. Anderson started, sitting cross-legged in the middle of our circle. "Today we're going to learn how to relax."

"Hey, no problem," yawned Tim, looking very much like a rumpled bed. "At last, something I'm good at."

Since I'd joined the group, I'd found out Tim is the youngest of four brothers; his older siblings are star athletes and honor students. He calls himself "the runt of the litter." It's sad to see him act like they're already too far ahead for him ever to catch up. Rebecca told me that he once admitted he was a bed wetter.

"It's not that easy for everyone to let go," Ms. Anderson explained. "You'd be surprised how much work it is for some people to relax."

We spent the next half hour lying on mats with our eyes closed. Ms. Anderson instructed us to imagine we were in our favorite place, a place that always made us happy. She told us to breathe in through our noses to the count of four and then exhale through our mouths to the same slow count of four, all the time picturing ourselves in our special place.

I was one of those people Ms. Anderson was talking about, much better at completing a task than floating away. Instead of sinking into the mat as Ms. Anderson suggested, I moved back a few feet behind the circle so my shoulders and neck wouldn't disturb the others. I concentrated on ticcing silently, praying I wouldn't spoil the exercise for everyone else.

I opened my eyes a little and peeked around. Jesyca could have been doing an impression of Sleeping Beauty. Her blond hair was fanned out like a halo around her head. Her little diamond stud earrings sparkled in the dark, accompanying the rhinestone heart on her shirt. As if this vision weren't nauseating enough, she had the nerve to actually have a very pleasant expression on her face. I still didn't know what had brought Jesyca to the Lunch Bunch. My guess was that she was hollow inside. But even if that was the case, I didn't feel at all guilty snarling at her profile in the dark.

I think Evan was snoring. Jon seemed to be giving it his best shot also. Clyde's brow was furrowed; just like him to try so hard that the effort made it impossible to let go. I started to feel guilty, remembering I'd neglected to call him back twice in the past week. Then, before my eyes, I saw him latch on to some idea that did the trick. His whole body seemed to melt and his breathing grew deeper. I wondered where he was. I wished I were there with him.

I started thinking about what had happened last Sunday. Rebecca and I had gone to the mall to buy bathing suits. While we were walking through the stores, the mall's air-conditioning broke. In minutes the heat was oppressive.

"Do you want to leave?" I asked, turned off by the thought of trying to slide a bathing suit on my sweaty body.

"You hot?" Rebecca said with a wicked smile. She looked straight ahead at the huge waterfall in the center of the mall. "Come on, let's cool off."

Before I had a chance to answer, she headed straight for the waterfall. Without a moment's hesitation she stepped over the ledge and walked under the water. In an instant she stepped out, dripping wet. She sat down on the bench and wrung out her hair.

"Your turn," she ordered.

If I hesitated one second, I knew my life would be more complicated than if I just plunged in. I looked around, took a deep breath, and walked under the waterfall. The water felt great. I stepped out and joined

Rebecca on the bench. In seconds we were laughing so hard I couldn't catch my breath.

"What's the matter, no umbrella?" There, standing directly in front of us, were Clyde and Jon. Clyde was still carrying his leftover popcorn from the movies.

"What's the matter, no guts?" Rebecca shot back.

"I'd rather have no guts than no brains," Clyde replied.

"Yeah, you probably would." Rebecca shrugged, standing up.

I sat there, a dripping mess, frozen in my spot.

"Well, are you coming?" she asked expectantly.

"Sure," I muttered as my sneakers made a squishing sound on the marble floor. I forced myself to look at Clyde, flinching even before I met his gaze.

He looked so hurt I had to look away.

"See ya on Monday," I said lamely as I followed Rebecca to who knows where.

I tried desperately to twitch the memory from my consciousness before my sounds could disturb the whole class. As I sat up to try to quiet myself down, I was startled to see Rebecca sitting in the corner, her back against the wall, searching through her bag for a barrette. Our eyes met and she pretended to yawn. I raised my eyes to the ceiling to show her I agreed with her. This was stupid.

Ms. Anderson's voice softly brought the class back to room 27. Then she asked us to go around the circle and share our favorite place with the rest of the group. Jesyca's was the beach, of course. I could imagine her spraying tanning oil on her flat belly in between the two halves of her tiny bikini. Jon's was swimming in the lake behind his grandma's summer cottage upstate. Evan talked even more slowly than usual, explaining his favorite place, sitting in front of a fireplace after he and his family went skiing last winter. Just as it got to Clyde's turn, Rebecca started whispering in my ear. Everyone could see she was not at all interested in where Clyde went to unwind. Even though I was, I continued to listen to her. She started to talk about a new move she wanted to try in dance class. I couldn't believe how rude she was, but I just nodded, hoping she'd shut up soon.

The bell rang, ending the discussion. I folded my mat and put it away.

"I'm sorry I missed what you said." I heard Rebecca ask, "So where do you go off to relax?" I turned to see her talking to Clyde.

He shrugged. "What do you care?"

"I really don't," she responded sweetly. "I was wondering if you already knew what to worry about after the mosquitoes quit for the year."

Clyde stared at her, trying to figure out what it was she was saying.

I felt my neck stiffen.

"Well, the Discovery Channel did a story about this death star that kills off most life-forms on earth every twenty-eight million years." Rebecca stopped and walked closer to Clyde. "The impact of the collision darkens the sky with dust, destroying all plant and animal life." She smiled this phony smile. Then, putting her arm on his shoulder, she continued. "It last hit twelve million years ago, so I figured that should give you enough time to obsess."

I felt my whole body tighten as my brain warned of an impending attack. This one began on all fronts. My eye started twitching just as the coughs started. As I raised my arm to cover my mouth, my shoulder cracked loudly enough to stop them both for a second. They looked at me, then started round two.

Clyde spoke first.

"You're right. I am always interested in frightening things," he said calmly. "Like the fact that Carrie actually thinks you're a nice person." Without giving her a chance to answer, he turned and abruptly left the room.

"Ooh, good one." Rebecca laughed without smiling. Then, without another word, she walked away and left me standing there.

What was with her? Why would she go out of her way to make Clyde feel bad? If I thought it was jealousy that made her act so mean, I'd still think she was wrong, but at least I'd understand. But why would Rebecca be jealous of Clyde? This was for sport. She should pick on someone her own size.

I looked up to see Ms. Anderson making believe she was straightening the mats. It was obvious she had been listening to every word. She caught my eye and transferred a ton of information in that glance. Although I wasn't part of the exchange, she knew it was all about me. And how I would react was important. My cheeks flushed.

"Wait up," I yelled, following Clyde down the hall.

Clyde kept walking.

"Come on," I pleaded. "She should never have said that, I'm sorry."

"Why are you apologizing for Rebecca? Forget it. That's just her warped sense of humor."

"All right," I sighed. I gave him what I hoped was my most pitiful look. "Just tell me what you were thinking about back there that relaxed you. I was twitching like crazy and wishing I knew where you were hanging out."

Clyde stopped walking. He turned to face me. "That's pretty ironic. I was at Burger King. With you, after we saw *Shrek*. Remember when we were laughing so hard at the jerks behind us?"

Of course I remembered. We were so hysterical that soda came out of my nose. I felt horrible that his best memory was a time he shared with me. And just as horrible that I'd come up with nothing. My face flushed as I recalled what had happened last Sunday at the mall.

Just then, my nose recalled something on its own. . . . It was time to start snorting in the immediate planet.

16

"All right, people, this is crunch time." Ms. Anderson had gathered the whole cast onstage. "We have only ten more days till show time. That means just six more rehearsals to transform today's basically good production into one deserving a standing ovation. Are we ready?"

The cast cheered. I looked around and found Clyde standing off to the side. Although he was clapping along with the rest of the kids, he looked preoccupied. We hadn't spoken since our conversation after lunch. I took a deep breath and walked over to him.

"Hey," I said in an overly enthusiastic tone, "what's up?"

Clyde stared at me the same way I look at Jesyca when she sounds loopy. Then he shook his head. "Nothing new is up, Carrie. What do you want?"

I shrugged. "Just trying to start a conversation. Could you be any nastier to me?"

"Listen, I don't want to be nasty to you. I just think that maybe we should stop pretending that we're still the same kind of friends we were, you know?"

Now it was my turn to stare.

"I mean, you spend a lot of time with Rebecca now and that's fine with me. You just can't expect to use me whenever she's not around, that's all." He gulped hard and then said, "I'm not mad. Just go, okay?"

I stepped back and nodded, not really sure what I was agreeing to. Had I just admitted that I liked Rebecca better? Did I have to choose between them?

Just then Ms. Anderson called for a run-through of a scene from act two. This was one of my few big moments in the play. I had to walk downstage alone and sing a few bars of a really sad song before the rest of the cast joined me. It was definitely my favorite part.

Everyone quieted down. Josh, who played the man I was supposed to marry, started his lines. I was getting ready to reply when all of a sudden my throat clogged up. Automatically I cleared it. Big mistake.

Josh finished his lines. It was my turn. I cleared my throat again and started to speak. Please, please, not now, I prayed silently. The cast waited. After just a few words, my head started jerking really fast toward my shoulder. Everyone stood quietly. The music started, signaling my solo. I walked down to my mark and opened my mouth, but the only sound accompanying the music was me furiously trying to clear my throat.

"Make it stop!" my brain screamed, but the Tourette devil just smiled. Then my mind went blank.

Ms. Anderson fed me the first line of the song from her seat in the front row. Although she smiled encouragingly, her face showed her concern.

" 'When I look into your eyes,' " I croaked before dissolving into a throat-clearing, head-jerking fit. Right there, center stage. You know how they say people who are about to die see their whole life flash before them? Well, I wish that's what I saw. Instead, I saw everyone else onstage looking at each other as if trying to figure out whether I was dangerous or just crazy. Then someone behind me muttered, "Oh, great, now what?" Whoever he was talking to just snickered. Then more people began whispering.

The music continued without me. I stood, fists clenched, eyes filled, no longer able to even see Ms. Anderson in the first row. There was no way I could go on. The murmuring grew louder. How stupid I was to think I was safe anywhere. Tourette didn't care that performing was my favorite thing, that I had been in every play since third grade. How stupid of me to believe I could continue doing something I loved as if I were normal.

I spun around to face the stage. "If I could think of how to explain to you what this is like, I would. I'm sorry to mess up your rehearsal."

With that, I jumped off the stage and ran to the back of the auditorium.

"Carrie, wait right there," Ms. Anderson commanded. Then she turned to the cast. "The rest of you sit, just where you are."

Slowly she walked down the aisle, back to where I was standing. She sighed and shrugged. "When people don't understand something, that's how they act. Like jerks, to cover up their nervousness." She held out her hand. "Come back. Let's try to explain things to them."

I shook my head and plopped into a seat on the aisle. "I can't."

"Yes, you can," Ms. Anderson said firmly. "Besides, you have no choice. The show is next week and we have to get this ironed out."

I stared at her in disbelief. Did she really think I was going back up on that stage?

"Come on," she insisted, this time pulling me up out of my seat. "You don't have to say anything now, just walk back with me."

Red-faced and sweaty, I followed her. By this time my head was jerking violently.

When she got to the first row, she clapped her hands. "I'm asking for your undivided attention," she said loudly, silencing the cast. "Would that I could permanently cure you of laughing at someone else's discomfort," she began in a low voice, "but maybe more information will help."

I sat down in the second row and put my hands over my face. No way could I look up at the dozen pairs of eyes staring down at me.

"How many of you have been in a play before?" Ms. Anderson asked.

Almost everyone onstage raised their hands.

"You know how whenever we change scenes, people in the audience cough. It's almost unconscious. They know that while the play is going on, it would be rude to disturb the others, so they wait until there's a break. Then they're able to let out the coughs they've saved up in the preceding twenty minutes."

I peeked through my fingers and watched as the cast listened intently.

"And you know how hard it is," Ms. Anderson continued, now pacing back and forth before the stage, "if you have to keep a secret from somebody, say there's a surprise party for them planned for the weekend, to keep yourself from saying, 'See you Saturday'?"

I never remember the auditorium so silent. I was surprised to see Jon standing in front of the curtain. He never comes out from behind his stool backstage. His eyes, usually looking down at the floor, were darting all over the place, from me to the rest of the kids to Ms. Anderson. He looked so upset, like he was absorbing what I was feeling, as if this were happening to him too. That's one of the things we experienced in the Lunch Bunch group. Empathy, Ms. Anderson called it. I had learned that although Jon's problems are different from mine, my misery is a familiar feeling to him. In the middle of my agony, I was touched.

Then I looked around, trying to find Clyde. He must have been hiding behind the curtain. I wondered if that was because he wasn't brave enough to look at me.

"Well, imagine if, through no fault of your own," continued Ms. Anderson, "you couldn't postpone that cough or keep from blurting out that secret. How much harder would that make your life?" She stopped pacing and folded her arms, looking each cast member in the eye.

Some people looked down; others started whispering. Ms. Anderson let them go on for a minute.

"Carrie has a neurological condition that sometimes doesn't let her stop herself from moving her head or her shoulder or clearing her throat. She tries, but these movements are uncontrollable." Ms. Anderson put her hands on her waist. She waited a long moment, then continued in a low voice. "I'm in awe of the job she does. I'm in awe of how she doesn't let Tourette Syndrome interfere with her participating in the play. I'm not sure if I were her whether I could handle it as successfully as she has. And she has never made one excuse or asked for one bit of extra consideration."

I peeked through my fingers. Now more kids had

their heads down. Probably for the first time in history, Jon's head was the only one that was up. He was looking directly at me. I sat up a bit straighter.

"I'm going to ask Carrie to forgive us now for making a miserable moment so much more difficult." Ms. Anderson turned to me and smiled. "Then I'm going to ask her to take her place onstage and continue from where we left off."

My heart started to beat double time. Was she out of her mind? Get back up there? I sat paralyzed. Then I saw Clyde walk out from behind the curtain. His eyes grabbed mine, like he was possessed, willing me to forgive him for upsetting me, begging me to join him onstage.

I pulled my eyes away and for the first time allowed myself to notice the rest of the cast. A few smiled sheepishly. One or two raised their eyebrows and nodded, as if repeating Ms. Anderson's request. Even the kid whose words had unnerved me looked sorry.

In spite of myself, I smiled back. I took a deep breath and stood up. What did I have to lose? The worst thing that could ever happen just had. Besides, I couldn't stand the idea of giving up my part.

"All right, I'll try again," I said, making my way toward the front of the auditorium. Jon walked to the edge of center stage, squatted down, and put out his hand to help me up. He looked very serious and didn't return my small smile.

"Thank you," I whispered as he walked, head down, back to his stool behind the curtain.

No one ever sounded less confident. I took my

place and Ms. Anderson cued the music. Then something I can't explain happened. It was as if a fog lifted and the path was clear. I glanced down at Ms. Anderson, closed my eyes, and began singing. I don't think I ever did as good a job. When the rest of the cast joined in, even they sounded better than they ever had. The rest of the rehearsal went on without a hitch. And without a tic.

I was exhausted at six o'clock when it was over.

"That's a wrap," Ms. Anderson called out. "Thank you, everybody, for all your hard work." She said that every day at the end of rehearsal, but today it felt different. Then suddenly one person started to clap. In a few seconds everyone joined in. I looked around to see what had happened. It took me a few seconds to realize I was the person they were applauding.

Again, without warning, my body reacted. This time, though, it was more appropriate. My eyes ran over with tears. I motioned for everyone to stop. Someone handed me a tissue. As I made my way to get my stuff, Clyde appeared alongside me.

"So what's new?" he asked with a grin. He bent down to pick up my jacket, then held it for me to stick my arms in.

"Not much, what's new with you?"

With that, Clyde was off and running, just like old times. He told me about the town's plan to hire two entomologists, bug experts, to treat all the ponds in the area.

"They have this fish called gambusia," he went on excitedly, "that controls the mosquito population by eating the larvae." He stopped, I guess waiting for me to faint over this information.

"Wow," I said, giving him my best impression of someone really knocked out by the news.

"I have a good feeling about this," he mused as we walked home together. "I think we have them licked."

As my grandma would say, "From his mouth to God's ears" to licking all the "thems" in our life.

17

If Ms. Anderson ever asked us to share the time we feel the loneliest, I would have to admit it's when my parents close their bedroom door each night. It used to always be open . . . before Tourette. When I was really little, my mom would come rushing in every time I coughed more than once. I can still remember making all kinds of phony sneezing and coughing sounds just to get her into my room. It was easy. She was a light sleeper and the door was always open.

As I got older, I can remember a million nights I ran to their bed after a bad dream. Without a word my father would lift the covers and make room for me to nestle under his arm. Sometimes I tiptoed in when I couldn't fall asleep because of a test or because I was too excited before a family vacation. And there were other times, if I got up to go to the bathroom in the middle of the night, when I would go in just to listen to them breathing. To make sure they were still there.

Then one night last fall, after I stopped taking the medication, they began to shut their bedroom door. The first night I remember was the night I started clearing my throat with such a vengeance, it got raw. I got up to ask my mother for a cough drop, figuring I'd get her to make a cup of tea with honey, when I noticed that the door was shut. At first I thought it was because of, you know, privacy issues. Then when it was shut the second night, I figured it was a precautionary measure so I couldn't hear them talking about me. But by the third night, I knew. They needed the door closed because listening to my noises drove them crazy. I needed to fit in that crook in my father's arm more than ever, but that spot was no longer available. Tourette Syndrome had seen to that.

If only we could have talked about it. But somehow it was as if they had read in some book that any expression of concern or worry on their part would be a bad thing. I never heard them talk about my Tourette with their friends, the way I'm sure they would have if I had any other kind of physical problem. If they couldn't fix it, then they'd pretend it wasn't happening.

• • •

"So have you seen Simon Trask recently?" my dad asked at dinner. I searched his face to figure out what he really wanted to know.

"Yeah, last week, why?" I answered while dishing myself some asparagus. I thought back to how evil the man had been.

"It's funny that you ask about him just as I'm about to eat this," I said, pointing to the green vegetable. "You know what Mr. Trask told me about asparagus?"

Mom and Dad looked up expectantly. Clementine was already smirking.

"He said no food makes your urine smell so bad so fast."

"What a guy," Clementine said. "I'll bet there's so much a man with his intellect could teach us all."

Simon had come home around four o'clock that Saturday, all windblown from a ride in his convertible. He wore a baseball cap backward on his balding head, one that said SEX, no less, like some homeboy wannabe. His suit was all wrinkled and he held up his pants with suspenders with skulls on them.

"Hey, Simon," Rebecca called out. "Hard day at the office?" She barely looked up from the TV. We were trying to learn the hip-hop moves of the background dancers in a new MTV video so we could bring them into jazz class.

"Where's your mother?" he growled, ignoring her question. He paused for a second when he noticed me, not that he acknowledged I was there.

"She's at a baseball game with Michael. She'll be back in an hour. Are you hungry? You want me to make you some lunch?"

"Nah, not now." With that, he walked upstairs to his room and slammed the door.

"Fred Friendly," I muttered, returning my attention to the video. I thought it was strange that Rebecca offered to make him lunch, like she worked for him or something. You'd think a grown man could put together his own sandwich, but I kept silent.

"He's a creep," Rebecca agreed, "but at least he's a rich creep."

I stared straight ahead. There is not enough money in the universe to make up for Simon's atrociousness.

"He didn't come home last night, so my mom's all upset. She was really hoping this would work out."

Just like that. Rebecca was talking about her entire world possibly being destroyed for the millionth time and she spoke as if she were discussing what she was wearing to school Monday. I wished she would tell me how she really felt. That's what friends are supposed to do. But there was something in the way she stuck out her chin as she shared this information that made me afraid to ask any questions.

"That's too bad," I said, trying to match her tone. It wasn't as if I could offer any advice. What would happen was beyond any kid's control. I just couldn't understand how Rebecca could be so blasé about it.

"You want to go to the movies?" she said, jumping up suddenly. "*The Stalker, Part Two* just opened yesterday." Before I could say how much I hate scary movies, she was on her way up the steps. "I'll get some money for the tickets and a cab from Simon. It'll be worth it to him to get us out of the house."

I shut off the television and thought of all the things I would rather do than see that movie . . . like have the doctor give me an injection with a big, long needle or have Mrs. Davis give us ten hours of homework. I knew Rebecca would just laugh at me if I told her how I hated feeling scared. I was miserable.

Then I heard loud talking from upstairs.

"How come you couldn't find yourself a normal friend?" I overheard Simon ask. "That head thing she does, it gives me the heebie-jeebies."

"Oh, stop being such a baby," Rebecca replied, lowering her voice. "You get used to it after a while."

"Not me. I deal with enough wackos during the week. I'd choose my friends more carefully if I were you," he advised. "Who you hang with is a reflection on you. Spend time with freaks and soon people will start staring to find out what's wrong with you; you'll see."

"Don't worry about me," I heard Rebecca say. "I can handle it."

My stomach dropped. I was the "it" she could handle.

A second later she bounded downstairs.

"See," she said triumphantly, a twenty-dollar bill in her fist. "Let's get out of here."

I didn't say a word during the whole ride. I prayed for the movie to be sold out. As Rebecca babbled on about how awesome the special effects were going to be, I was planning my strategy. I'd just get up a lot during the movie to go to the bathroom and get popcorn so she wouldn't notice how much I hated it.

My luck, we got right in. The only seats left were right in the middle of the third row. That meant I'd have to bother at least eight very loud, obnoxious teenage boys every time I got up.

As soon as the lights dimmed, I knew I was in trouble. My body gave me the two-minute warning that it was as unhappy as the rest of me that we had to sit quietly for the next hour and a half. As my back stiffened, I tried desperately to figure out my survival plan. We had just sat down. It was too early to disturb the boys. Besides, I had to use my trips sparingly.

"You thirsty?" I asked Rebecca.

She shook her head. "Not yet."

I concentrated hard, praying to postpone the onset of my tics. Most of the time, once I got into a movie, they quieted down. But this was a film I didn't want to concentrate on, one I hoped I'd be able to stare at and not see. Simon Trask's words intruded. Then I lost the battle. It started with some fairly innocent throat clearing. The boy next to me glanced over, then turned back to the movie. I was so preoccupied with keeping as quiet as I could, I had no idea what was happening on the screen. Rebecca was enthralled the moment the opening credits were over. I thought about Clyde. If I were sitting next to him, he would feel me tense up instantly, even without looking at me.

I coughed a few times, attempting to pretend I had a cold.

"Shhh," whoever was behind me hissed.

"You want a hard candy?" Rebecca asked, unconscious of what was going on.

"No thanks, I have," I whispered, popping one into my mouth. Maybe there would be a miracle and the magic candy would stop my noises. Yeah, and I'm Miss America.

The coughing continued. It seemed like an hour but the movie was just beginning. People around us started squirming.

"Keep it down."

I dug my nails into my sweaty palms, trying to focus on my breathing as Ms. Anderson had suggested. Inhale to the count of four, then exhale to the count of four. Empty your mind of everything but the breath going in and out of your nose, she had instructed. The problem was that my mind refused to clear, insisting instead on dwelling on how annoyed the kid next to me was getting.

When I couldn't bear it anymore, I leaned over to Rebecca.

"I'm going out to get a drink," I murmured.

She nodded, barely acknowledging me.

As I stood to squeeze out of the row, someone sitting right behind us groaned.

"Don't come back anytime soon," offered one of the boys as I stepped on his foot.

"Jeez, can't you make her stop?" I heard the kid

next to Rebecca ask. "I can't concentrate on a freaking word with all her coughing."

I was too busy concentrating on avoiding the soda cups and popcorn tubs to make out her answer.

"Well, I'm going to call the manager if she keeps it up," he continued, loudly enough for me to hear. "I paid to see this movie, not hear her cough to death."

Head down, I made my way up the aisle to the lobby, giving up on any measure of control. There wasn't a person in the theater who didn't hear me leave. My vision blurred, making me feel like I was going the wrong way down a one-way street. When I reached the lobby, I leaned weakly against the wall opposite the candy counter. As the throngs walked in and out of the multiplex, my breathing finally came closer to the goal Ms. Anderson had suggested. After a while I even stopped sweating. Then the coughing subsided.

I was zoning out, wondering how long it would take Rebecca to realize I'd never come back, when I felt someone tap me on the shoulder. It was Jesyca. The fun never stops when you're me, I thought.

"Hey," she said, "are you okay? I came out to buy popcorn about an hour ago and I noticed you standing here. Now I'm back 'cause I gotta go to the bathroom and you're still in the same place. Do you feel all right?"

"I'm fine," I said. "I'm not a big fan of scary movies." I opened my bag, pretending I was taking out money to buy something at the candy counter. "I was just headed back in," I lied.

"Okay, then." Jesyca smiled, her tone revealing she didn't believe a word I said. She wasn't smart enough to fool me. "I'm sitting with my brothers in the next-to-last row on the left if you need anything." Then, suddenly looking as if she was afraid she was overstepping her boundaries and making me angry, she scurried away. When she reached the bathroom door, she looked back at me one more time.

For some reason I couldn't figure out, Jesyca's concern made me feel worse. When Rebecca found me there after the movie ended, she didn't say one word. Neither did I. Not that I had wanted her to miss the movie and come check to see that I was okay. Only, of course, I had expected she would.

It's weird, my friendship with Rebecca. We do fun things and dance and shop, but she pretends to ignore my Tourette the way I pretend to ignore her family life. It's so different from my relationship with Clyde. When Clyde and I choose not to discuss something, we're still on the same page. With Rebecca, I'm not even sure if we're reading the same book.

18

"When you plant lettuce," Ms. Anderson began the day's Lunch Bunch discussion, "if it doesn't grow well, you don't blame the lettuce. You look for reasons it's not doing well. It may need fertilizer, or more water, or less sun. You never blame the lettuce."

I was sitting next to Rebecca in the circle. Clyde was on the opposite side. I tried to catch his eye, but whenever Rebecca was in the room, he wouldn't look at me.

"Yet if we have problems with our family or our friends, we tend to blame the other person. I believe if we know how to take care of our relationships, they will grow well, like the lettuce."

Oh, great, I thought, that figures. Somehow it was up to me to figure out how to forgive Rebecca. What was so crazy was that she had no idea she'd done anything wrong. I kept thinking she was ditzy and that's why she was completely unconscious of what I'd gone through, waiting in the lobby for more than an hour for the movie to end. But how could any kind of friend not even ask where I'd been?

I tried concentrating on Rebecca's good points. She's pretty and smart and doesn't let what other people think bother her. It's great having someone to practice different dance combinations with. And I love the creative way she says things, like that the sand the plows poured over the snow last winter reminded her of crumb cake. She always acts like my tics don't matter at all. In a strange way maybe that's the problem . . . they probably should matter, at least a little.

The discussion droned on, but I didn't pay much attention. Evan talked about how it's his mother's fault that his dad left because she got this new job and worked too many hours and he didn't like having to do her job at home. Ms. Anderson just nodded, but I could see there was plenty she didn't say. Jesyca told how her sister failed out of college and now because her parents wasted a whole year's tuition, they can't go on vacation this summer. And Jon spoke about how mad he was at his mother, who, since his grandma died last year, just sits home and cries all the time.

"Okay," Ms. Anderson said, clapping her hands, "enough. It's time for a change of pace." She looked at Clyde and nodded. He nodded back. "Ladies and gentlemen," she began, sounding like the ringmaster of a circus, "I'd like to introduce you to the president of our school's newest service club, Clyde Paskoff."

We all looked at Clyde. He stood up slowly and began distributing stickers that said BITE FIGHTERS!

"Last week when I was on my computer looking up the latest information about West Nile virus, I found out the department of health was looking for kids to help educate the community about the *Culex pipiens.*" He stopped to catch his breath.

We all knew from Clyde that that was the real name for the common household mosquito. He kept us updated weekly on the number of cases of West Nile virus on Long Island. I'd never seen him so excited before.

"I volunteered to start a group in our school," he continued. "There aren't many opportunities in life for kids to protect their families from a deadly disease." He waited for his words to sink in. The group was definitely interested.

"The enemy is standing water," he went on, his voice gathering strength from our undivided attention. "I'm asking for volunteers to help eliminate the places where mosquitoes breed."

"My mother won't let me go near any swamps or marshes," said Jesyca.

"I wouldn't ask anyone to go there," Clyde replied.

"Ninety percent of the breeding goes on in our backyards. I need people who'd be willing to give up some time on Saturday mornings to let their neighbors know that if they sweep any puddles off their driveways and throw away any containers that hold water, they can reduce the risk of thousands of mosquitoes being born." He looked around and stood a little straighter. "I have a list of the information that needs to be given out and badges for anyone interested. . . ."

Five hands shot up, including Jesyca's. Clyde smiled broadly. He didn't even notice that my hand was not one of them. Or maybe he did and didn't care.

"The first meeting is at my house at eleven this Saturday morning. We'll break up into committees for making posters, removing old tires, talking to the other classes, and clearing leaves out of storm drains."

"Can I be in charge of posters?" Jesyca asked. "I'll bring over all my art supplies and stuff."

The whole group started talking at once.

Clyde's face was flushed. It was amazing to see him transformed into this powerful leader right before my eyes. Ms. Anderson looked at me and grinned. She knew how happy I was to see him feel this way.

The bell rang. Everybody gathered around Clyde to ask him some questions. Rebecca came up behind me.

"How goofy does that sound?" she asked, rolling her eyes.

"I don't know," I said slowly. "I think it's probably a good thing they're doing." That was the best I could do on the spur of the moment. I couldn't allow her to dis Clyde's idea, but I couldn't let myself be part of it, either.

"Whatever." She shrugged. "I'll speak to you later." Then she raced out the door.

I saw Clyde watch us out of the corner of his eye.

"Can we walk home together?" I asked lightly, ignoring his frosty glance. "I want to hear more about all this." Part of me felt bad that he hadn't told me about it before. But Ms. Anderson's lettuce story was still fresh in my head. I could understand why he hadn't.

"Not today," he answered curtly.

"Why not?"

"My mother is coming up after school to talk with Ms. Anderson about what we do in Lunch Bunch." His voice sounded agitated.

"Oh." I fought a surge of panic. "Did your mom make an appointment?" It had never entered my mind that my parents might get a call.

He shook his head. "Ms. Anderson called yesterday. I probably would have told you, but I was busy organizing all this stuff and didn't get off the computer till ten-thirty. Besides," he said, his voice softening a little, "I didn't want to worry you. Maybe she only phones the parents who don't understand their kids."

"Like mine do?" I groaned. Then I took a deep breath. Maybe there was something to what Clyde said. He was still obsessed with all this mosquito stuff. As far as Ms. Anderson knew, I had made a new friend and hadn't had an episode that she'd witnessed since the play rehearsal.

That's what I was thinking about on my way home. It was a beautiful day, but I scarcely noticed. All I kept thinking about was what would happen if Ms. Anderson called my house. A loud buzzing broke my concentration. I lifted my head just in time to walk into a swarm of mosquitoes. My first thought was Thank God Clyde isn't with me. My second thought was *Ouch* as I slapped my cheek hard, catching a mosquito midbite. Then I waved my hand in front of my face because another one of his pals was going back and forth, searching for a juicy spot to land.

Suddenly the inside of my left elbow began itching. I pulled up the sleeve of my T-shirt and dug my nails into the skin. If Clyde had been standing there, he would have been totally convinced my time was up. Whatever that mosquito left inside me was already floating in my bloodstream. At this very moment, it was getting its bearings, asking directions to my brain.

Although it must have been seventy-five degrees outside, I shuddered. Get a grip, I mentally yelled to myself. This is Clyde's craziness, you have your own. My head hurt. Then I remembered the West Nile thing starts with flulike symptoms. I searched my mind for a statistic, any statistic I might have spouted to calm Clyde down. Only 1 percent of those bitten by infected mosquitoes get the disease. One out of a hundred. My breath grew more regular. By the time I got home, I had my facts straight. Mosquitoes were pesky insects with the irritating habit of biting people. They were not killers.

At home I put calamine lotion on my two bites and thought about how easy it was to get carried away, and how awful it had been to be in Clyde's skin for a few terrified minutes. Being that frightened by all kinds of things was probably no easier than having Tourette.

19

"Okay, class," Mrs. Davis began, "we have fifteen minutes till lunch. Let's see how well you've learned how to use the different research techniques we've been working on all year. Using any sources available, I want you to find out how many presidents have their faces on coins and dollar bills. The first person to come up with the right answer will be excused from doing tonight's homework."

The class buzzed and then raced to the back of the room where the computers and bookshelves are. I took my time. Now, if she had said the first person to answer correctly wouldn't have to take the next math test, I'd have been right on it. As it was, speedy research is not my strong point, and the homework at this time of year is no big deal.

By the time I reached the books, the most helpful ones were gone. I picked up the C volume of the old encyclopedia and thumbed through it, heading toward the back to look up currency. I was stopped by the page headed COLLEGES. There, right in front of me, was a list of the colleges all our presidents attended. To my amazement, there were eight who had never graduated. My heart started beating. Clementine would love this. I grabbed my pen and hurriedly copied down their names: Grover Cleveland, Millard Fillmore, Martin Van Buren, Zachary Taylor, Andrew Jackson, Andrew Johnson—and surprise of surprises—George Washington and Abraham Lincoln.

"All right, time's up," Mrs. Davis called out.

I didn't even listen to the correct answer. What I had found made me happier than being excused from homework for a month.

• • •

"Why didn't you call me back last night?" I whispered to Clyde later that afternoon. He had avoided looking at me all morning and had stayed far away during Lunch Bunch. I knew how excited and busy he was with his new project, but still . . .

"I'm sorry. Jon and Tim called about Saturday morning and then I had to print out an outline for our first meeting."

It wasn't that I wasn't interested in the Bite Fighters. I mean, I really was happy that Clyde was doing something besides worrying about his problem, but right now all I cared about was what had happened at the meeting between his mom and Ms. Anderson.

"It's going to be great, I know it," I said in my perkiest voice. "Oh, by the way, what was that meeting like between your mom and Ms. A.?"

I saw in an instant he didn't buy my "Oh, by the way."

"It was fine," he said, not looking up from his paper. "She told my mom how great it is that I'm heading up the Bite Fighters club and how, since I've been practicing relaxation exercises, I seem calmer about my fears." He raised his two pointer fingers in the air to trace quotation marks when he said "fears."

I waited, hoping he'd continue.

"My mother was all smiley in school, thanking Ms. Anderson for her help in Lunch Bunch and with the play, but when we got home, I heard her tell my dad she thought the school psychologist should be trying to get me to go out at lunchtime instead of coddling me."

I shook my head. Clyde's parents have a son who gets A's, who's the lead in the school play, and who has the kindest heart, and all they talk about is that he's afraid of mosquitoes.

"So since when are you too busy to call me back?"

Clyde looked uncomfortable. "As my mother was leaving, Ms. Anderson complimented us . . . you and me . . . on the kind of friendship we have. Then she said she was going to be calling your parents today to set up a meeting." He looked up at me and sighed. "I'm sorry I'm such a coward, but I hated telling you and I figured you could use another night's sleep before you heard."

Ta-da, the trumpet sounded, awakening my body to the crisis ahead. Only, the way my body prepares for a crisis is the exact opposite of helpful. My fingers started drumming on the desk. Then my shoulder began begging to be cracked.

"Carrie, will you collect the signatures of the seventh-grade teachers now?" Mrs. Davis asked. "I don't want you to miss the science lesson I cooked up for later."

Perfect, I thought, holding my breath to remain silent till I reached her desk and picked up the folder. I needed air. Closing the door behind me, I looked down the empty hallway. Then I shuddered, majorly, from head to toe. Usually I have time to get to the girls' bathroom, but not today. Five days before the play and my parents are getting a call about the Lunch Bunch. I was trapped. I couldn't ask Ms. Anderson not to call, because as far as she was concerned, they knew about it. She could get into trouble if I didn't have parental permission. Clementine would catch hell.

I could see dinner now. Mom would act like she'd lost her best friend. Somehow the fact that I hadn't told her would be all about her, not my reasons for keeping it quiet. And Dad's jaw would be racing the four-minute mile. My sister would be cool, but I still felt terrible about the lecture she would have to endure. I knew I wasn't cut out for this forging-signature stuff. I flashed on how Rebecca would deal with this. She could convince her mother that tomorrow was a new school holiday and never get caught.

I practiced inhaling and exhaling through my nose to the count of four. Ms. A. swears that focuses your thoughts and helps to reduce stress. In this case, an oxygen mask might have been more helpful.

I tried not to think about dinnertime too much for the rest of the day. It wasn't like I had the power to swerve and avoid it. I just had to keep steering in the direction of the skidding car and wait to see what would happen. I was pretty sure I'd live through the collision; I just didn't know about surviving the waiting.

That afternoon we were scheduled to run through the whole show without stopping. There was a different feeling in the air as it hit us that the performance was only five days away. Rebecca said she was really excited to see it. She was even bringing her little sister. Clementine was coming with her latest boyfriend. It was a good thing, I convinced myself, to have to concentrate on my lines.

The show started without a hitch. I was waiting backstage to go on, listening to Clyde finish his first song. He was so good. I peered out to see if Ms. Anderson was smiling. What I saw made my knees buckle. There, sitting in the first row right next to Ms. A., was my mother! What in the world was she doing here? Sometimes parents come by to drop off dinner or pick their kid up early for a doctor's appointment, but never to just sit there and watch like my mom appeared to be doing now.

The music started and it was my cue to walk onstage. I took my place, ignoring the front row. Clyde and I had this scene where his character disapproved of what mine was doing and I had to answer him in a nice way. His eyes fastened upon mine, forcing me to keep looking just at him. I took a deep breath and got into the scene. As long as my eyes never left his face, I was safe.

"Hold up," yelled out Mr. Gelb, the music teacher who played the piano for us. "Sorry, I've got to run out to my car for a second to get the sheet music for the next song."

"No problem, take five," Ms. Anderson directed. "Great start, everybody."

My mother stood up and waved. She motioned for me to come down into the audience.

"I'm right behind you," murmured Clyde. "Let's go."

"Hi, Mrs. Peller," he began, reaching my mother before I did. "What are you doing here?"

"Oh, Dr. Schneider had emergency surgery and we had to close the office early, so I thought I'd surprise Carrie."

Mission accomplished.

"What a weird coincidence that you came by today." Ms. Anderson smiled. "I was going to call you tonight."

"Oh?" my mother asked. "Is there something I can do to help? Do you need me to assist backstage? I was stage manager of the drama club in college. . . ."

"No thanks," Ms. A. said, "I think we've got things under control. I was calling to set up an appointment to speak to you about Carrie."

"Carrie?" my mother said, still unconcerned. She looked at me and grinned. "She's a great kid, isn't she?"

I stared at the floor. Just let the guillotine fall already.

"Yes, she is," Ms. Anderson replied warmly. "This is about the Lunch Bunch. I always connect with the parents of the kids involved at least once during the year."

My mother knit her brow. "I'm sorry?"

"The Lunch Bunch," Ms. Anderson repeated. "Carrie has added so much to all our discussions. She's a terrific problem-solver."

I saw the moment when Ms. Anderson understood my mother had no idea what she was talking about.

"Let's leave those compliments for another time. Is next Monday afternoon good for you?" she continued smoothly.

My mother's smile weakened. She nodded, then turned to me.

"Places, everyone," Ms. Anderson yelled out. "Let's go."

I shrugged and burst out, "I gotta get back onstage, Mom. Why don't you go home?"

My mother stiffened.

"It's just that it makes me a little nervous, you sitting there. I'd rather you see us when we're perfect. It's only five more days." I pleaded. If I had to do the show with her staring accusingly, I couldn't go on.

"Okay," Mom said shortly. "I'll see you at home." Then, turning to Ms. Anderson, she said, "And I look forward to seeing you Monday."

I watched her walk out of the auditorium. Even from the back she looked upset. I felt like following her, apologizing for embarrassing her in front of my teacher. She didn't deserve that. Just as I didn't deserve to have to perform right now. We'd see just how good an actress I really was.

"Think happy thoughts . . . ," Clyde muttered under his breath as we took our places onstage. "Remember, the more upset you get, the worse your tics will be."

Ms. A. had been working with all of us on how much worse whatever hurts us is when we're under too much stress.

But even as I listened, a tic wrenched its way out of my throat. It was too late to escape by counting the wood planks on the floor. I had to ventilate my brain by letting off the pressure building inside. I ignored the sounds coming out of me and went on with my lines. When it came time to sing, I disregarded my head jerking. This was a run-through. Nothing would be gained by my stopping. A new tic-and-gesture combo was born onstage that afternoon, a sort of foot-flex, heel-raise thing that wouldn't quit. Clyde's eyes widened; then he sighed. He understood.

The cast knew my tics meant no harm, and they continued around me. I looked at the clock . . . 4:15. A little less than two hours left of rehearsal.

20

Sometimes music calms me. I went straight up to my room after rehearsal and put on the radio. A song came on, from one of those boy groups who are prettier than most of the girls I know. I flopped down on the bed and stared at the ceiling, waiting for my mother to call us for dinner. I was only home thirty minutes, but it seemed a lot longer. Have you noticed how slowly time passes when you're waiting to be yelled at, especially when you don't have any idea of exactly how angry your parents actually are?

My wait wasn't too long. There was a knock on my door, followed a second later by my sister bursting into the room. She held her ears and wrinkled her nose, signaling me to turn off the radio. Romantic songs sung by boys who use hair spray offend Clementine.

"So how did they find out?" she asked, as if we were already in the middle of a conversation. "I just overheard Mom telling Dad that you joined Ms. Anderson's therapy group without asking their permission."

It figures my mother would call it a therapy group.

She plopped down next to me. "I had all my faculties when I agreed to forge their signature. Don't worry about telling the truth. I can handle them."

Whatever else you could say about my sister, you could never call her predictable. I would have thought she'd be furious. I was prepared to tell my mother I'd signed her name, but I was relieved to share the blame.

"I don't want to get you in trouble," I started unconvincingly. "It's my lie; I'll tell them."

"You're right, it is your lie, but I'll accept my responsibility in aiding and abetting such a horrible crime," Clementine said.

"Thanks," I said gratefully. "I'm really nervous about this."

"Just be honest. Mom and Dad will never understand why you asked me instead of them unless you explain it."

She was right, of course. How glad I was at that moment to share something that I knew would please her.

"Before we go downstairs, what would you say if I told you I had eight more names for your door?"

Clementine just blinked and said, "Cool. Who?"

I ran to my book bag and pulled out the paper with the names. "Grover Cleveland, Millard Fillmore, Martin Van Buren, Zachary Taylor, Andrew Jackson, Andrew Johnson . . . ," I recited, then stopped for effect. ". . . George Washington and Abraham Lincoln."

Clementine's eyes widened. "Are you sure? That's amazing!"

I handed her the list. "Technically, none of them completed four years of college," I said proudly.

Just then, Mom called out, "Girls, dinner's ready." I listened carefully but didn't hear anything in her tone to help prepare me for what lay ahead. What a waste, I thought as the aroma of dinner, meatballs and spaghetti, wafted up the stairs. It was my favorite meal, but I couldn't imagine eating.

"Let's get this over with." I sighed.

Clementine put her arm around me as we walked out of my room. "Remember, the problem here is that they don't understand. And that's not entirely their fault."

Mom and Dad were already sitting at the table. They looked at each other, then each forced a smile, pretending nothing was wrong.

"Did you smell what I made for dinner?" Mom asked.

You would think it would make me feel better, knowing they weren't out to get me. Instead, it made me furious. I stood behind my chair at the dinner table and began to speak.

"I never told you about the Lunch Bunch because I thought you'd get all upset," I burst out, "and anyway, at first I only joined because of Clyde."

They both put down their forks. Clearly, this was not how they'd expected the conversation to start.

My foot started tapping. "He wouldn't go outside at lunchtime because of the mosquitoes and so I figured this was a way we could stay inside without hiding." The words spilled out in a rush. "I know that was wrong, but sometimes it's just easier not telling you things than to deal with how freaked out you get."

"Your father and I decided that you must have a reasonable explanation—" Mom began.

"And now that you tell us you were only trying to be a good friend," Dad interrupted, "I think a promise that this will never happen again should end the matter."

There it was. Over. All I had to do was say "I'm sorry" and I was home free. So why was anger flowing like lava into my throat?

"Can I say something?" Clementine took her seat, folding her arms across her chest. "All I keep thinking about is Uncle Sam."

Uncle Sam was my mother's uncle. He was a sweet old man, about eighty, and the only legitimate hero in our family. He lost his leg in World War II, parachuting out of an airplane behind enemy lines.

"You know when we take a photograph of the whole family, how Uncle Sam stands behind a plant or a chair so no one looking at the picture will realize he's missing a leg?"

We all nodded, waiting for the moment when it

would become clear what the heck she was talking about.

"You two do the same thing with Carrie's Tourette," Clementine said, lowering her voice. "She knows you prefer looking at her from behind that chair, so she hides there." Clementine's cheeks were all red. "The fact that she never tells you what hard work it is to be her . . . don't you ever think that's a little strange?"

I felt tears sting my eyes. I jerked my head sideways, then turned it slowly as if I were working out a kink.

"Is your sister right? Is that how you feel?" my father said, playing with his napkin. His eyes were down, staring at his empty plate.

Clementine smiled into my eyes encouragingly. "Tell them," she ordered.

I was still standing, my hands clenched in tight fists at my sides. "Yes."

My mother swallowed hard. "I ask you every day how school was, and you never say a word." Her voice broke.

"It's not all your fault," I said, walking around to take my seat. "I should have been able to talk to you. But you both seemed to be having such a hard time with my tics, I didn't want to complicate your life any more."

"Hard time?" my dad questioned, raising his chin in my direction. He still didn't look at me, though. "Like how?"

Was he kidding? It was time to tell him "like how."

I'd let out my feelings like I let out my tics. The words poured out.

"Like letting that disgusting Mr. Trask talk to me so rudely without saying a word," I spit out. "Like pretending you don't see me when I start ticcing. Like clenching your jaw whenever my shoulder cracks. Like closing your bedroom door to keep me out when I need you both so much."

Although my voice was strong, I felt sick inside. I could barely catch my breath, but I couldn't stop now.

"And you, Mom, you don't act embarrassed like Dad does, but you behave like my tics are just this minor annoyance. If I tell you I had a bad day, you take it personally, like it's your job to make it better." I took a deep breath. "It's not. Sometimes all I want is for you to listen and not say anything."

My mother seemed to look straight into my heart. "I'm so sorry," she whispered. "You're right, of course. No one hears your tics louder than I do. And every time you make those noises, I die inside. I'm so ashamed because all I want to do is scream for you to stop."

Her hands were shaking as she picked up a glass of water. After a long moment, she continued. "I'm so worried that if I lose patience so easily, how must the rest of the world be feeling? If I asked you . . . and you told me . . . every rude remark and insensitive look, I'd want to go out and strangle each one of them. A mother is supposed to protect her children from anyone who dares to hurt them. But with this"—

she gulped hard—"Tourette Syndrome, I feel so helpless. . . . I wish this had happened to me instead of you."

I felt a lump form in my throat. I saw how hard it was for her to even say the name. There was more my mother wanted to tell me, I knew, but she was trying to do as I asked.

"I did join the Lunch Bunch because of Clyde," I went on, her distress giving me confidence, "but now I see that I belong there too. It's good to be in a place where you don't have to be afraid to say what's really on your mind. Where it doesn't make a difference if you're beautiful or bug crazy or a mess of tics."

"I'll look forward to talking with Ms. Anderson," Mom said quietly. She glanced at my father, but he was looking down at his hands clasped on the table. His shoulders slumped forward and he looked like all the helium had gone out of his balloon.

"At the office I always tell people that a divorce, like a serous illness, has a ripple effect," my father began, his voice so low we had to lean closer to hear him. "That it never happens to just one person. It affects everyone who loves you." He cleared his throat and was quiet for a long moment. "I had to make believe I was fine with your Tourette." He swallowed hard. "Shame on me for handling this so badly."

He looked up for the first time and his voice grew stronger. "I need some time to think about what you've said. And what we can do to make it better. Is that okay?"

I nodded. Now *my* shoulders were slumping forward.

"The thing of it is," Clementine reasoned, directing her remarks to my parents, "how lucky are we that we get away without sharing Carrie's burden? She lets us off the hook. We pretend to believe that it's not so bad or she'd complain more, because that's what we would do. I think we should admit we could never handle Tourette as well as Carrie does."

The table was silent. Suddenly I became conscious of the smell of meat sauce. I inhaled deeply, surprised to realize I was starved.

"So, Carrie," my mother implored, "are we okay?"

Before I had a chance to answer, my father did.

"No," he said softly, looking at me for the first time, "but we will be."

21

That Monday, after collecting the attendance sheets, I stopped off at Ms. Anderson's office. Before she met with my mother, I felt it only right to tell her about the signature. She was so cool she made confessing a lie something I could manage without counting every square tile in the hallway.

Unless she was sitting and talking to someone, Ms. Anderson's door was always open. She glanced up from some papers she was reading and smiled. I wondered how she could look so happy to see me, especially since we spent lunch hour and every afternoon after school together.

"I'm so glad you stopped by," she began, shuffling

the papers around on her desk. "I found this new study that backs up what we were talking about last week, about how we don't have to let tension make us sick—"

"I only have a minute," I interrupted, "but I wanted to talk to you before you met my mother."

Ms. Anderson raised her eyebrows but didn't say a word. She leaned back in her chair and gave me her full attention. I'd never realized how rare it is for someone to do that . . . stop doing whatever they're doing and focus only on you. My sister does it, and so does Clyde when he's not in mortal danger.

Ms. Anderson remained silent, even after I finished telling her about Clementine signing the note and what happened at dinner. Watching her made me want to learn how to hear people the same way.

"Every single person in the world has something in their lives that's hard to deal with." She sighed. "And the problem only gets worse when we try to make it go away by either fighting it or ignoring it."

Rather than jump in and defend myself, I copied Ms. Anderson's body language and waited for her to finish.

"We have to accept our problems and realize they're all part of being human, like curly hair or a birthmark. Everyone has their differences. You can't stop shrugging your shoulder or clearing your throat any more than you can change your fingerprint."

I liked that comparison.

"What you did at dinner was show your parents

you trust them. By telling the truth, you gave them a chance to be more honest with you too."

She reached across the desk and put her hand over mine.

"I'm not ever going to lie to you. There will always be those ignorant souls who can't handle your behavior. But that's their problem. The ones worth caring about will learn the difference between bad behavior and neurobiological disturbances." Then, as if she read my mind, she said, "Just because they're your parents doesn't mean it's automatic."

I thought about how long it had taken before my mother and father finally stopped arguing with Clementine about burning incense and how she wears her hair.

"Thank you," I said thickly. "You're really good at what you do." I stood to leave, then sat back down again. "Can I ask you one more question?" Without waiting for an answer, I said, "It's about Rebecca."

Ms. Anderson raised her hand, signaling me to stop.

"Let's leave Rebecca for another time," she said with a smile.

"I'd rather not," I answered, surprised by how strongly I felt. If I was already into this therapy thing, I might as well get it all out. "If you have the time, I'd like to talk now."

"Okay, shoot," Ms. Anderson said, sitting back in her chair.

She listened as I rattled on. When I finished, she sighed and rubbed her eyes.

"If I were to ask you what makes the Lunch Bunch work, what would you say?"

I paused to get the right words out, but the answer was easy.

"I think because we're all honest about what it feels like to be scared or guilty or embarrassed; we trust each other. Knowing we're all in the same boat makes us care about people we might never have noticed before."

"That's it exactly." She nodded. "Feeling what other people feel is very hard for Rebecca. Opening herself up, taking that risk, is not easy when you haven't had much opportunity to be a child."

I thought back to the awful stories Rebecca shared. And how when she told them, it was as if she were remembering someone else's life.

"There's a price to pay for pretending you're capable of handling anything one hundred percent of the time," she said softly. "It's not her fault she's not the friend you want her to be." Then she clasped her hands in front of her on the desk and straightened up. "That's all I feel comfortable saying about Rebecca right now."

"Thank you," I said as I stood to leave. This was a new thought, that an unsophisticated misfit like me could understand a concept that cosmopolitan Rebecca didn't. Empathy.

When I reached the door, Ms. Anderson added, "Oh, by the way, your father called this morning."

I stood with my hand on the doorknob.

"He told me what happened at dinner and asked

if he could join your mother this afternoon at our meeting."

I shook my head. "You knew the whole story and you didn't stop me."

"I knew his story. I wanted to hear yours."

"And?"

"And you're very lucky, Carrie, it was the same story. No blame, no excuses. I give him a lot of credit. It's not easy picking up the phone and admitting you're wrong to a stranger."

I left school psychologist's office and slowly walked back to my classroom. My dad was going to leave work and come to the meeting. He was really serious about trying to make it better. That was very good news.

22

The day of the performance I came home at 5:30 just to drop off my books and pick up my costume. It wasn't easy to be in a hurry and avoid every single crack in the sidewalk. But someone was on my side. I made it home in one trip, without having to start all over again. Lucky, because I was due back to school in half an hour.

My dad was on the phone in the kitchen when I came through the door.

"Tell Mr. Trask it's Bob Peller."

I stood frozen at the foot of the steps.

"Yes, he knows who I am. Tell him I'll be happy to remind him if he forgot."

I never remember hearing my dad's voice quite so

edgy. I put my book bag down and sat on the bottom step. My stomach was in knots. What had happened in Ms. Anderson's office? What did he want with Simon Trask?

I heard my father inhale deeply while he waited. He was pacing back and forth. The refrigerator door opened and closed. Then the conversation began.

"Yeah, hi," my dad began. "Thanks for taking my call."

Simon spoke and then I heard my father's voice change.

"Well, it's not business or pleasure, exactly. I thought I might run into you this evening at the school play. Carrie has a big part and I'm sure Rebecca will be there."

He paused. "Oh, I figured you might be picking her up afterward. . . ."

Simon obviously had no idea what my father was talking about. I couldn't make out the words he said, but he spoke loudly enough for me to hear that he sounded annoyed.

"Listen, in all honesty, it makes no difference to me whether you're there or not. I have to get something off my chest and it might as well be now."

He paused.

"You remember when we met outside your home? For whatever the reason, I chose to look for excuses for your incredible rudeness and lack of sensitivity toward my daughter."

"Don't raise your voice to me," my dad said quietly. "This will just take a moment. I sat in my car that day and let you embarrass Carrie because I was impressed by your reputation and your financial success. Also, I know how much she was looking forward to going into the city to celebrate Rebecca's birthday and saw her disappointment when she was suddenly disinvited. Carrie never told me why, but I can imagine."

I heard yelling on the other end of the line. The louder he yelled, the stronger my father's voice sounded.

"Of course it's my business; your actions have hurt my daughter. I'm calling to say that as long as Carrie and Rebecca are friends, I will expect that you keep that ugly mouth of yours closed. If I find out that you've said or done one more thing to hurt Carrie, I'll come up to that big, fancy office of yours and make sure I share my feelings with as many people as possible."

I heard my father sit down to listen to the tirade directed toward him. After a minute he broke in.

"I really wish I had more time to continue this conversation, but I have to go. No, I haven't threatened you. I've warned you to find someone your own size to pick on. If you can find such a person." Then he hung up.

I leaned back into the wall. My heart was beating double time. I stood up and tiptoed upstairs to my room. I only had a few minutes to get my things together. There couldn't be a worse time to think about what I'd just heard. Then my phone rang.

"Carrie, what just happened?" It was Rebecca.

"Wh-what are you talking about?" I sputtered.

"I just got off the phone with Simon. He's furious at me. He said your dad called to scream at him about how Simon treats you. What is he talking about?"

Any other time I might have felt sorry for Rebecca. I might have tried to understand why she was so angry with me. Why she blamed me for that monster's inexcusable behavior and why she couldn't realize how his words made me feel. But tonight was the show, and all I could think about was how selfish she was to lay this on me right now.

"Rebecca, the play starts in two hours. I can't talk to you about this." My voice was strangely calm, as if I were acting out another part.

"I'm sorry to bother you," she said icily, "but I've been defending you ever since we met. I thought you were mature enough to ignore him without being a crybaby. Now your father really did it. Simon's going to come home in a foul mood and take it out on all of us. Then my mom will blame me." She paused. "You just don't get it. I walk on eggshells around here making sure Simon doesn't get mad. And then your father—"

"I said I can't talk to you now," I interrupted, "but I'll tell you one thing. The rest of the world doesn't have to walk on eggshells, Rebecca. That's the deal you made, not me. I gotta go."

"Thanks for nothing," she lashed out. "I don't think I ever started a sentence this way, but Simon was right. He said if I don't watch it, I'll be spending my life taking in birds with broken wings." Then she slammed down the receiver.

Not once in the conversation did she ask, "Are you all right?" or "What made your dad call?" What if Simon was right and I was a bird with a broken wing? Rebecca would never comfort me. She couldn't even wish me good luck. Just thanks for nothing. I closed my eyes and directed vibes her way, mentally boomeranging her parting words right back to her. Then I put my things in a big shopping bag and ran down the steps.

A half hour later I was back at trying to put on my makeup. Ms. Anderson took one look at me and tried to calm me down. "You know what courage is, Carrie?" she asked. "Courage is fear holding out just a few minutes longer," she whispered in my ear. "No tic is going to be the boss of you. You are going to be great."

As she walked out of the room, she almost collided with Jon, who, head down, was walking in. She stood at the door and watched as Jon made his way to where I was sitting.

"This is my lucky shark's tooth," he muttered, stuffing a tissue into my hand. "My grandmother gave it to me when I was in first grade. I always bring it with me when I could use a little extra luck." He stopped for a second. "I don't know if you believe in this stuff or not, but . . ."

"Oh, Jon, who doesn't believe in luck?" I broke in, talking as fast as he did so he wouldn't see how moved I was. It was amazing. Jon is someone I never spend two minutes thinking about, but at that moment he knew what I needed better than anyone. I tucked the tooth, still wrapped in a tissue, in my sock. "Is this okay?"

"Great." He grinned.

I think it was the first time I ever saw his front teeth.

"Now for sure you're gonna kill tonight."

He was right. I did. It was a completely ticless performance. The fact that Clyde played my father made every word meaningful. Even the audience, which included most of the kids in our class, was perfect, giving us a standing ovation.

When the curtain fell, I grabbed Clyde and pulled him to the side of the stage.

"We have to talk. Can we go to the movies on Saturday after your meeting? I have so much to tell you." I was surprised at how nervous I felt.

"Sure. Why don't you come with us in the morning? We're sweeping all the puddles out of the driveways on Milburn Avenue." He wouldn't give me the satisfaction of smiling, but I knew he wanted to. Then he added, "I've got plenty of stuff to tell you too."

At that moment Ms. Anderson came backstage and everybody started cheering. She looked so happy.

"Good work, everyone. You did a masterful job." She caught my eye and smiled. "Bravo to the heroes among us," she said, pointing at me. Then she began to clap. In a second the entire cast was clapping with her. Clyde was clapping the loudest.

People started to leave to meet their parents and friends in the hallway. As I gathered my things, I noticed Jesyca standing at the back of the dressing room. She was carefully holding a small bouquet of flowers, encircled by her ten perfectly pink fingernails. Wetting her lip-glossed lips nervously, she looked pale and ill at ease.

"Hey," I called out. "Miss A. just left; you can probably catch her in the cafeteria."

Jesyca walked toward me, smiling shyly. "I'm not looking for her. I came to give these to you."

I stared at the flowers she handed to me.

"Don't say anything," Jesyca began in a rush. "I know you don't really like me that much. I don't blame you for thinking it's sick that I spend so much time worrying about how I look and what other people think of how I look. The truth is I agree with you." She gulped hard. "I hate seeing myself in a mirror as much as you hate that head stuff you do."

I would have interrupted her if I'd had a clue what to say. This was news. The stories Jesyca told during the Lunch Bunch might have revealed how ditzy and not-that-smart she was, but how could anyone with Jesyca's wardrobe, fashion sense, and beautiful hair not like what she sees in the mirror?

"I just wanted you to know," she continued, speaking very fast, "that if I had your brains and your confidence, I wouldn't be worrying about what I wore all the time. I have to work hard on the outside because I'm not strong like you are on the inside." She paused, suddenly embarrassed. "Anyway, I just wanted to tell you, you were amazing tonight."

I felt flattered and confused and guilty all at once. Who ever would have thought I'd be having this conversation? I thought about that old saying "You can't judge a book by its cover," and for the first time understood why old sayings live on through the years.

"Thank you, Jesyca," I said as I reached to give her a hug. "You have no idea how good you just made me feel."

Her wide grin told me she knew I meant it.

• • •

It was on the ride home, after my parents gave me their flowers and took pictures, after Clementine told me how my acting had made her cry, after I dug Jon's lucky shark's tooth out of my sock, after I spoke to Clyde and told him about Jesyca, that I realized Rebecca never had shown up.

23

"Why did the blonde stare at the carton of orange juice?" Ms. Anderson began. It was the day after she had assigned "dumb blondes" as a topic for us to find a funny joke about. She said humor was a powerful tool for good and evil, and today we were seeing how it was used to create stereotypes. This subject was allowed, she said, since she—a natural blonde—had brought it up. She waited just a second before rewarding us with the punch line. "Because it said concentrate."

"What did the blonde call her pet zebra?" Tim called out.

"Spot," Clyde blurted out, delighted to finally get one. It was the last week of school and we were all a bit slaphappy.

"One of my little brothers told me this one," Rebecca offered. "It's the hottest joke in second grade. Why do blondes smile in a lightning storm?"

While the group tried to figure out the answer, I looked over at my former friend. We hadn't spoken since our phone conversation. She'd never asked about the play. I'd never asked what had happened with Simon. It wasn't just that the words we'd used were so hurtful . . . that happens all the time when people argue. It was that neither of us thought we were wrong. I certainly wasn't going to apologize, and obviously she thought she'd been absolutely right to attack me like she had.

"Give up?" she asked. "Because they think they're getting their picture taken."

It wasn't very funny, but we laughed anyway. Then Rebecca continued.

"I don't know if this is the right time but I want you all to be the first to know that I'm moving. My mother decided that the suburbs are deadly for business, so we're on our way back to Manhattan. Tomorrow."

There had to be a lot more to that story than a business location. How awful that she couldn't even stay four more days, until school finished. I tried to catch her eye, but she wouldn't look back.

"This group's been cool. Whenever any of you guys come into the city, look me up in the phone book. It should be listed. We're not running from anything this time." She sniggered.

The room was silent. Then Ms. Anderson said, "It

must be hard on you, moving around so much. Do you know where you're going to be living?"

"Not really. We're going to stay with my grandmother for a few weeks till my mother finds a place. It sucks, but I'm used to it." She shrugged, signaling the end of the conversation. Then she added, "The worst part is that you always have to be so careful about who to trust."

Instead of feeling attacked, I felt sorry for her. Why would they have to leave in such a hurry? I hoped my father's call wasn't part of the reason. I wondered whether she was referring to Simon or me. Or both of us.

The bell rang. I made sure to be the first one over to say good-bye to her. That way there'd be a line of kids waiting behind me.

"I'll always remember you," I said honestly. "Keep up with the dance classes. Maybe we'll meet at an audition one day." I felt dozens of coughs lining up like planes on a runway, anxious to leave my throat.

"Yeah, right," she answered. She looked behind me and smiled at Tim. I knew she thought he was nerdy and boring. "Thanks for all the laughs, Tim," she said with a hard edge he didn't pick up on.

I moved away. Suddenly I understood why she wouldn't trust anyone. The people in Rebecca's life come and go. It's too risky to care about anyone when chances are, before too long, you're only going to miss them. It hit me that the only time I ever knew for sure what Rebecca was feeling was when she called me up to scream about my father. That was one instance when she let down that protective shield she wraps around her emotions. She never—could never—let me in to share what scares her or worries her or makes her cry. For the first time I saw the holes in the thin layer of confidence she hides behind.

Instead of feeling hurt or angry at the way she'd said good-bye, I was just sad. She really had made a difference in my life. Aside from introducing me to the hideous Mr. Trask and making me dis Clyde big time, I'd always remember her for being the first friend I made after Tourette.

"You okay?" Clyde asked as we walked back to the classroom. Although I'd told him what had happened the night of the play, he realized that I still could feel bad that Rebecca was leaving. That's a friend.

"I'm fine," I said in between coughs. "Better than I would have thought."

"Good," he replied simply. "How're things at home?"

"Strange." Since our discussion at dinner, Mom didn't ask anymore about how my day was. She and Dad made it a point to be more conscious of my tics. Instead of ignoring them, Dad offered me a tissue or asked if I needed a drink. One night, after a particularly brutal shoulder-cracking episode, he knocked on my door and asked if it would help if he rubbed my back for a while. Mom went out of her way to make eye contact, just to let me know she was there. She told me she had contacted the other parents of the kids in the Lunch Bunch and they were all chipping in to buy Ms. Anderson a gift.

It was almost two-thirty when I realized I had

forgotten to collect the attendance records. We were in the middle of this neat science experiment, observing how ants organize their lives. I jumped out of my seat and ran toward the door. Mrs. Davis looked up.

"Is everything all right?" she asked.

"I was so involved with the lesson, I forgot to make my afternoon rounds. I'll be right back." As I reached for the doorknob, Mrs. Davis got up from her desk and walked out into the hall with me.

"There's something I have to tell you," she said with a small smile. "This job you've been doing so diligently"—she paused—"you can choose whether you want to continue or not."

I didn't understand.

"It was Ms. Anderson's idea to have you collect the attendance sheets. Usually we just hand them in at the end of the day, but she thought it would give you a perfect opportunity to leave the room whenever you needed to. She said she woke up one morning and there it was, the solution. Her only regret is that she didn't think of it earlier in the year."

I was flabbergasted. Two teachers had lied to me and made up a phony job? That meant all the teachers in the grade were in on it. My face felt hot.

As if she had read my mind, Mrs. Davis said, "It's highly unusual for us to go to such lengths, but you've always been so responsible and mature. We both wanted to figure out a way to help you handle your Tourette with the least trauma." She put her arm around me. "I don't blame you one bit if at first you're angry with us." She sighed. "Just promise, when you think this over, you'll imagine yourself through our eyes. Then you'll understand."

Without thinking, I put my arms around Mrs. Davis's waist and gave her a hug. She hugged back. "I'm a little embarrassed, but I'm a lot more thankful," I said. "I guess I never realized how much teachers care about their kids."

"Well, spread the word." She laughed.

"If you don't mind, I want to thank Ms. Anderson. I'll be back in a minute."

"Of course. I don't want to take the rap all by myself."

Mrs. Davis walked back into the classroom and I continued down the hall to Ms. A's office. Her door was wide open. She had emptied the contents of her top drawer onto her desk and was sorting through them.

"Excuse me, can I have your attendance sheet?"

Ms. Anderson looked up, perplexed. "My what?"

"Your attendance sheet," I repeated. "Yours is as important as any of the others I've been collecting for the last two months."

She didn't know what to say. Ms. Anderson, with all her studies and exercises and jokes, was speechless. She lifted the hair off her forehead, I think to better see my face and figure out if I was kidding or really upset. "I'm not a big advocate of lying, Carrie, you know that, but this was the whitest of white lies. You needed an escape route. This was one you could custom-make to fit your habits. It was a judgment call. Were we right?"

I smiled broadly, letting her off the hook. "How can I ever be angry with you? You've been so wonderful to me . . . and to all the kids. Did you notice that Clyde wore shorts this week? It was those clippings you showed him about the amount of money the county is spending to clean up the breeding grounds—that did it."

"No, I think it was a combination of things . . . the play, the group, and the fact that he feels he got his best friend back."

I came around behind her desk and gave her a hug. I was getting good at this teacher-appreciation thing. "His best friend is never going anywhere. Who else would put up with us?"

Suddenly Ms. Anderson got all serious. "Speaking of friends, I've been meaning to ask you, are you all right about Rebecca? I watched you both carefully for a long time. In my opinion, your relationship was at least as important to her as it was to you, no matter what she might have said."

Leave it to Ms. A. to teach, explain, and soothe all at one time.

I walked back to my class without having to make my usual bathroom stop. There was so much to think about. I flashed on the new addition to Clementine's door. There, right under Millard Fillmore, it read MY SISTER, CARRIE. It was hard to accept that that was real.

Clyde and I walked home slowly.

"So did you hear that the president allotted money to make sure this doesn't happen again next year?" Clyde asked, assuming I knew what he was talking about, which, of course, I did.

"So what will you be afraid of next?" I asked, only half joking.

"I'm not sure," he answered with a straight face, "but who would I be without something to worry about?"

I smiled, knowing just how he felt. I knew something else too. That while occasional turbulence might throw us off course, Clyde and I would be fine. After all, there wasn't a broken-winged bird in sight.

AUTHOR'S NOTE

While Carrie is a fictional character, her struggles and triumphs would be very real to thousands of children whose lives are complicated by Tourette Syndrome. If you happen to know someone in school who exhibits some of the behaviors Carrie does, you may hesitate to ask questions for fear of embarrassing them. Even if you don't know anyone like this personally, chances are that somewhere along life's journey, you will cross paths with someone whose behavior puzzles and confuses you. Just as a little knowledge helped Clyde cope with his fears, having a few questions answered may make your encounter with such a person richer.

1. What is Tourette Syndrome?

Tourette Syndrome is a neurological disorder that is characterized by tics, sudden movements or noises that a person has little control over and that repeat many times throughout the day. Someone with this condition may be able to postpone an outburst, but eventually the urge is irresistible and the behavior must be expressed. The type of tic and how frequently it reappears often changes over time. Sometimes symptoms disappear for weeks or months.

2. What do these tics look like?

Tics can include blinking, repeated throat clearing or sniffing, arm thrusting, kicking, shrugging, and jumping, among many other actions.

3. What causes the symptoms?

No one really knows. Scientists suspect it has something to do with two chemicals in the brain, dopamine and serotonin.

4. How can a doctor tell if you have Tourette Syndrome?

The doctor relies on observing a patient's symptoms and learning as much as she can about when the symptoms began. No blood test or neurological test is available yet to diagnose Tourette for sure.

5. What are the first symptoms?

The most common first symptom is a facial tic such

as blinking or mouth twitching. Sometimes throat clearing or sniffing comes first.

6. Are there medicines to treat Tourette Syndrome?
Most people with Tourette do not require medication. For those whose symptoms are severe, there are several medications to choose from. Unfortunately, some have undesirable side effects like weight gain and fatigue. Seeing a psychotherapist can be helpful, as can learning relaxation techniques to deal with the stresses that cause tics to increase.

7. Is it important to treat Tourette Syndrome early?
Yes. Sometimes parents, teachers, and friends see a person's symptoms as bizarre and frightening. As a result, someone with Tourette may be left out of activities and prevented from enjoying normal relationships. To prevent more psychological harm, early diagnosis and treatment can be very helpful.

8. Are there any other problems associated with Tourette?
Yes. Many people with Tourette also have:

[a] obsessions, unwanted and bothersome thoughts that run constantly through the patient's mind.

[b] compulsions, which make a person feel that an act must be performed over and over or in a certain way. Sometimes a child with Tourette will ask her parents to repeat a sentence many times until it "sounds right." Sometimes the child needs to touch an object with one hand after touching it with the other to "even things up." Sometimes she checks and rechecks for reassurance that the stove is turned off or the door is locked or her homework is in her book bag.

[c] attention deficit disorder (ADD). Many people with Tourette have difficulty concentrating or finishing what they begin. It's tough for them to listen carefully, and they become restless and fidgety.

[d] sleep disorders, frequent awakenings and walking and talking while asleep.

9. Does Tourette Syndrome have anything to do with how smart you are?

No. People with Tourette have the same intelligence range as the rest of the population. Some have learning disabilities, however, which may make solving math problems, taking timed tests, and writing harder.

10. Is Tourette Syndrome inherited?

People with Tourette have about a fifty percent chance of passing on the gene to each of their children. The chance is three to four times higher that a son will express symptoms than a daughter.

11. Is there a cure?

Not yet.

12. Does Tourette ever go away?

Many people get much better in their late teens and early twenties. As many as a third of patients see their tics diminish greatly or in some cases disappear in adulthood.

13. How many people have Tourette Syndrome?

Because many people with Tourette haven't been diagnosed, there are no accurate figures. Studies do indicate that approximately 200,000 Americans have the classic symptoms of the disorder. Many people have tics, but not necessarily Tourette.

SOURCE: THE TOURETTE SYNDROME ASSOCIATION

If you have any other questions, you can contact the association at
42-40 Bell Boulevard
Bayside, New York 11361-2820
(718) 224-2999
www.tsa-usa.org